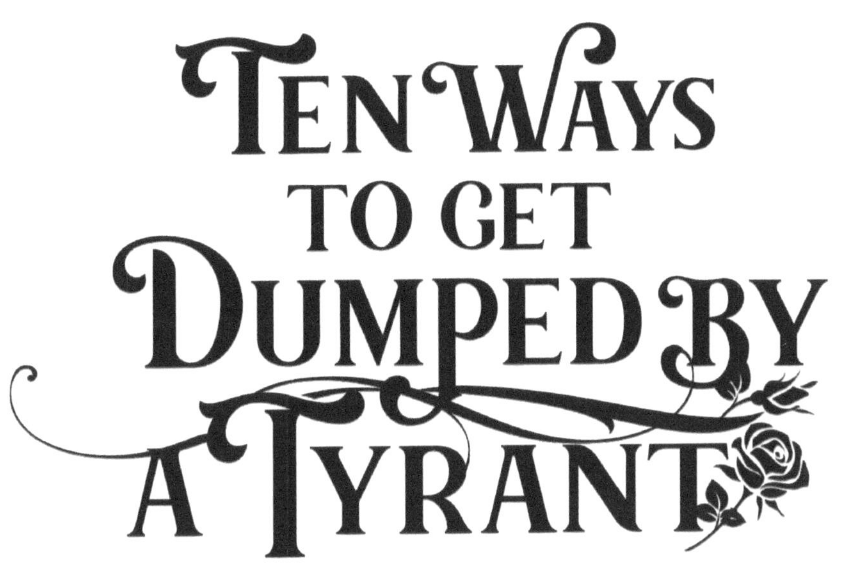

TEN WAYS TO GET DUMPED BY A TYRANT

폭군에게 차이는 10가지 방법

WRITTEN BY SEO GWIJO

EDITIO

PUBLISHING

Ten Ways to Get Dumped by a Tyrant

CONTENTS

Chapter One Hundred and Twenty-One 1

Chapter One Hundred and Twenty-Two 9

Chapter One Hundred and Twenty-Three 19

Chapter One Hundred and Twenty-Four 28

Chapter One Hundred and Twenty-Five 36

Chapter One Hundred and Twenty-Six 45

Chapter One Hundred and Twenty-Seven 53

Chapter One Hundred and Twenty-Eight 62

Chapter One Hundred and Twenty-Nine 71

Chapter One Hundred and Thirty 81

Chapter One Hundred and Thirty-One 91

Chapter One Hundred and Thirty-Two 101

Chapter One Hundred and Thirty-Three 110

Chapter One Hundred and Thirty-Four 119

Chapter One Hundred and Thirty-Five 127

Chapter One Hundred and Thirty-Six 136

Chapter One Hundred and Thirty-Seven 147

Chapter One Hundred and Thirty-Eight 156

Chapter One Hundred and Thirty-Nine 165

Chapter One Hundred and Forty 176

Chapter One Hundred and Forty-One 186

Chapter *One Hundred and Forty-Two* 196

Chapter *One Hundred and Forty-Three* 206

Chapter *One Hundred and Forty-Four* 216

Chapter *One Hundred and Forty-Five* 227

Chapter *One Hundred and Forty-Six* 236

Side Story *Chapter One* 248

Side Story *Chapter Two* 257

Side Story *Chapter Three* 266

Side Story *Chapter Four* 275

Side Story *Chapter Five* 284

Side Story *Chapter Six* 293

Side Story *Chapter Seven* 302

Side Story *Chapter Eight* 311

Side Story *Chapter Nine* 322

Side Story *Chapter Ten* 331

Side Story *Chapter Eleven* 339

ONE HUNDRED AND TWENTY-ONE

The very first thing I saw when I walked over was Charlemagne staring intensely at an unfamiliar woman with red hair as he spoke to her. I wondered what he said, because the woman blushed as she replied.

At the time, I did not even think that she might be Cheryl Diel.

I mean, her face looks different.

The face I had seen in the video wasn't as soft and gentle. Even her eyes, nose, and the corners of her mouth were different.

There's no way I wouldn't remember her face when I replayed that video countless times!

I was sure of it. This woman couldn't be Cheryl Diel.

"Your Majesty Charlé."

"Lady Lettie." Charlemagne smiled as he looked at me. The way his expression changed so dramatically was enough to cause misunderstandings.

He probably thinks of me more as a friend than a lover, though.

I had come to this conclusion after he had teased me in a way that made me wonder if he knew how I felt about him. Though I was sad, I knew this was for the best as he would feel that sense of destiny when he sees Cheryl Diel for the first time.

Feeling relieved that the woman in front of us wasn't Cheryl, I asked Charlemagne, tilting my head in confusion, "Hmm? Who is this woman?"

"I wonder?" he answered. "She's one of the many things that aren't worth your concern."

His smile deepened. It was so gorgeous that I could stare at it all day.

"Lady Lettie." As I stood there, speechless and blinking at his smile, he asked with a laugh, "Were you with that jerk... I mean, with Lord Masiar?"

He's acting like he's jealous or something.

Perhaps it really was jealousy. I just didn't know if he was jealous because he thought of me as his lover or as his friend.

In the original novel, Charlemagne used to kill people at the drop of a hat if he was jealous. Even though he was different after our journey inside the cursed book, people really never completely change. I knew he felt possessive and obsessive toward me, so it was obvious he'd be jealous, but that was it.

"Oh, yes, we had a very meaningful conversation."

"You did?"

Of course, I didn't want to see him chop off people's heads out of jealousy.

He tilted his head slightly. "What kind of meaningful conversation?"

"Yes, our little Glenn here…"

I could feel myself being the center of his attention. *You sinful man… I'm still a woman!* I'll keep deluding myself if he kept being possessive of me.

I hid my sulkiness as I finished my sentence. "…feels lonely sometimes."

"So, you comforted him." Charlemagne's sweet voice filled my ears, but then his tone cooled. "Does his personality take after his childish appearance?"

Oh, come on, that's mean. "Aw, Your Majesty. Even grown men feel loneliness."

Glenn wasn't too sensitive about comments on his looks, but he didn't seem welcoming of them either.

Or maybe not? He does use his looks to his advantage.

At that moment, the unfamiliar lady that I had almost forgotten about spoke. "It's very nice to meet you, Lady Arman." Her voice was delicate and graceful. Surprised, I turned to face her, and she lowered her eyes. "My name is

Cheryl Diel.”

What? My eyes widened in bewilderment. *What did she say?*

But before I could ask her to repeat herself, she smoothly moved her gaze away from me to focus on Glenn.

“Who might this person be?”

“Uhh, I am Glenn Masiar.”

Dude, hold up. She just said her name is Cheryl Diel!

She had red hair and green eyes, but she looked different from the Cheryl Diel that I remembered in the video. It wasn’t even a subtle alteration. She looked totally unlike the woman I saw in my old memories. No one here knew her face better than I did.

Everyone else here had no interest in her until she appeared, but I had watched those videos so many times.

Unable to read the room, our little Glenn said stupidly, “It... it is an honor to meet someone so... beautiful.”

“I’m flattered, Lord Glenn.”

As I turned to look at Glenn at his ridiculous statement, Cheryl’s smile snagged my gaze. Unlike her altered appearance, that smile was the very one that I remembered.

What the hell is going on? Why did her face change? I mean, I didn’t influence that by being involved in this world.

I was mystified.

"It is the truth..."

On hearing Glenn's nonsense, I whipped my head back around. Charlemagne's eyes flashed as he watched me silently. There wasn't anything positive, like curiosity, in his eyes. They were drenched with something close to bloodlust.

"Are you displeased?" he asked me quietly.

"About what? Glenn?" I answered just as quietly.

He nodded, and a somewhat playful smile began to bloom on his lips.

"Not really. More than that, it truly appears that he doesn't know her."

I had thought that Glenn might feel something if he met her in person, even if he didn't know anything about her. He had felt something strange when he looked at the estate, so I'd been almost certain he would, but...

A thought sparked in my flustered mind, and I stepped closer to Charlemagne.

"You know, Your Majesty..."

"Hmm?" He leaned his ear toward me like it was the most natural thing to do.

Not even realizing that it looked like I was in his arms to the others, I whispered, "Can dark wizards change their faces?"

"They could, but I would have felt it if she changed her face with magic. That's her real face."

"Huh?" *Does that eliminate my disprove theory that Cheryl Diel is a dark wizard?*

"What about her face?"

I paused and gazed at Charlemagne. He didn't know Cheryl's face from the novel. "She looks a bit different from what I remember."

"Hmm." He looked over at Cheryl, and my mood darkened as I watched his persistent gaze.

Come to think of it, he had been standing close to her earlier. I mean, it wasn't like he didn't know anything about her. I did tell him I saw her in my dreams. I even told him there was something suspicious about her. But his expression wasn't even... that murderous.

I could feel it. He was focused on her, but not because he wanted to kill her.

At that moment...

"Yaaawn."

"Chancellor Clover..."

"Ugh. Why don't you call me something more informal, Lord Glenn? Add 'Your Excellency' or something, for example." Chancellor Clover approached us, stretching.

I hid my bad mood as I whisked around to look at him instead. "Are you done resting?"

"No, Lady Scarlett, I'm not. I need more rest, but what

can I do? Life doesn't flow the way I want it to... But who is this?"

Before I, the person he was talking to, could say anything, Cheryl butted in. "It is very nice to meet you, Chancellor. My name is Cheryl Diel."

Ew! Jerk! I was starting to really dislike her.

"I live in that castle you can see over there."

Honestly, when I saw her up close, she was stunning. The hand that gently brushed her hair away seemed so pure yet so seductive. I watched with an odd expression.

"Ah, I see," said the chancellor.

"I left my estate by myself because this place is usually safe from monsters, but then..."

"Aha..."

She is pretty, but her personality has changed, too.

As I watched her suddenly loosen her tongue in conversation with the uninterested chancellor, I felt that something was off. Her personality was more upright and honest in the novel. Right now, she was as innocent and lovely as a newborn fawn.

As I was absorbed in their conversation, Charlemagne's hand brushed my cheek. I jumped and turned to look at him, and he removed his hand as though he was satisfied.

"About what we said in private, Lady Lettie."

"Yes, Your Majesty. I'm glad you remember."

"Of course, I do. It happened only a moment ago."

"But then, why..."

Why aren't you on your guard? It's not like you. It was always obvious when Charlemagne was wary because he would give off threatening and deadly vibes. But he wasn't reacting that way.

"Hmm?"

I felt kind of glum, but as I was feeling sulky, the chancellor and Cheryl's conversation continued next to me.

"So, that was how I came to this place, and then I saw His Imperial Majesty in his godlike..."

Ugh, just look at them talk.

"Where is this wind coming from? And why is it only blowing over one person? Tsk."

"...form..."

"Ah, I apologize. I rudely cut you off. It was intentional, Lady Diel."

Huh? I blinked in a daze. *Their conversation sounds weird.*

CHAPTER
ONE HUNDRED AND TWENTY-TWO

Charlemagne, who had been watching my mood, drew my eyes to his.

"Intentional?"

"Oh my! My mistake again. I meant it wasn't intentional. Anyway, I'm quite hungry."

"I... I see, Chancellor."

I stifled my laughter as best I could. Cheryl's voice was exactly as I had remembered. It was shaking with unbridled fury.

"Yes, I feel like eating a late-night snack. This lady should return to her own lands now."

"That's all ri—"

"It's late, but there really is no reason for you to stay at such a place when your estate is so close, is there?"

Oh. My. God. This is so satisfying! Recalling the way she had cut off my words earlier, I gazed at the chancellor proudly.

Charlemagne watched me in silence before smiling brightly. He said in a low voice, "Lady Scarlett. You look like you're having fun."

"What? No, why?" *Of course, I'm having fun, but I'm not going to make it obvious in front of you!*

Because I thought he knew how I felt about him.

"And this wind keeps blowing too, you know? This goddamn wind! How come it only blows in your direction? You must treat your hair more preciously, Lady Diel."

That's right!

Cheryl didn't seem to be able to find words. She awkwardly shifted her eyes to look at all of us in turn, but sadly, none of us were courteous enough to offer her a place to spend the night.

"It truly is suspicious," Charlemagne muttered, but he wasn't whispering to me on purpose. As if the words slipped out of him without his realizing, he observed Cheryl, whose shoulders were shaking delicately like she was going to cry at any moment.

I didn't like the intensity of his stare, but I quietly watched her as well. "What is?"

If it weren't for my vision, she would have looked like a harmless—from my point of view anyway—and feeble young lady.

Right as Charlemagne was about to answer my discreet question...

Peep! Peeeep! A beautiful birdcall rang out.

"What is that?"

"It looks like a bird."

The spies hurried over to my and Charlemagne's side, exchanging hasty dialogue. The chancellor also came over, looking uninterested. Cheryl couldn't keep up with what was happening, so all she did was fume and watch us.

"Lettie! Lettiiieee!"

"It's shining!"

The babies—I mean, the fairy boys—who had been playing with my communication bead inside the tent, flew over, their cheeks flushed with excitement. I absentmindedly turned away from the bird and looked at them.

"Gill? Bell?"

"Look at this! It's pretty!"

Before I knew it, the blue bird fluttered over and flew around me, like it was performing a trick.

"Oh! Hmm? It's not actually a bird..."

It was light in the shape of a bird.

Bewildered, I stood still, and Charlemagne watched the bird with a serious look on his face. I had moved into his arms without even realizing it, but I was flustered only for a moment.

No, wait, he started it!

I pretended to be even more frightened and hugged him back tightly.

"Ugh," someone groaned overhead.

What was that for?

"O-oh, that bird scared me." I sounded like a robot, but it explained my reason for hugging him. "You make me feel safe, Your Majesty," I whispered as coyly and primly as I could.

"Uh..." He was speechless for some reason. All he did was slowly relax his body and take a few deep breaths.

Is he mad?

I was kind of hurt, but the moment my eyes met Cheryl's, who was looking at me like I was absurd, sparks flashed in them. I held on to Charlemagne even more tightly.

"Ahem..."

"Cough."

The spies and the chancellor glanced at me and Charlemagne as they cleared their throats awkwardly, still looking wary of the bird.

When my embrace tightened, Charlemagne's body stiffened again, and a slightly shaky sigh blew over the top of my head. I didn't want to let go, though.

I'm just scared, okay? He didn't have to be so repulsed by it.

As I sniffled a little, the bird silently landed on my shoulder and tipped its head to the side.

"Wha... Hey! What is that tiny thing?"

"Get off! That's our spot!"

Gill and Bell suddenly started bullying the bird as they flew toward me.

Peep! Peeeep!

"Go awaaay!"

Peep! Peep!

The boys pulled at the bird with their tiny hands, but the bird, being made of light, didn't budge, watching them silently. Just as the boys were about to cry, the bird twittered and...

"Oh!"

It rubbed its tiny head on my cheek.

"It's Baba."

"Excuse me?"

At the sound of Charlemagne's dark voice, I forgot I was depressed and jerked my head up. All I could see was the edge of his chin. He intentionally hid his face from me as he continued speaking.

"It's a mass of mana."

"Oh?" *This bird is a mass of mana? Is that possible?* No matter how uninformed I was about how this world worked, even I knew such a thing was impossible.

I wasn't the only one who had heard Charlemagne's words.

"Mana is just mana. It isn't a living thing."

"This bird looks like it's alive, doesn't it?" the chancellor and No. 1 inquired, disconcerted.

"And Baba's mana is pink. This bird is blue." I pulled myself away from Charlemagne slightly as I chimed in, and his eyes finally met mine. His face was no different than usual.

Then he wasn't nervous about my hug? He really was mad?

An odd sense of disappointment cascaded over me, and I became sullen again. I was so busy drawing hasty conclusions that I didn't realize his ears were bright red.

The chancellor groaned. "Tsk. My stomach is twisting again."

Charlemagne opened his mouth. "I don't know what it's for, but it's harmless."

"I see..."

At that moment, the fairies, who had been fighting with the bird, pounced on it all at once.

"Get off! Lettie is ours!"

Peeeep! Peep! Peep!

Sob. "Nell! Nell, come help us!"

Bell's tearful cry was followed by a tiny *pop,* and Nell appeared out of thin air.

"What in the world was that?"

"C-can the dear fairies teleport as well?"

"It's the first time I've seen something like this, too!"

"I took all the others home!" Nell yelled as he materialized.

Already?

"But why did you call me?" Nell cocked his head as he floated in the air, a tiny flower petal stuck to his face near his lips.

"This thing! With Lettie!" Bell and Gill shouted, acting bizarrely cross. "Get off!"

"What is that little thing, Lettie?" Nell was far calmer than the other two, but as he fluttered toward me, I could see that the lips that were mulishly clamped shut on his small face looked fierce.

Peeeeep! The bird chirped as though in protest when it saw Nell.

"It's ugly!" Nell huffed.

"Well, that's—"

"We're prettier! Right?" Gill shouted.

"Waah! Lettie! Hold us!"

"No, not you, bird! Just us!"

"Boys?"

What the... I'm starting to feel sorry for the bird! Why were they acting like this when all that bird had done was come sit on my shoulder?

The blue bird continued to prissily whisk its head away from the fairies, who looked like they were about to lose their minds as it dominated my shoulder.

"Lady Lettie doesn't belong to you." A gentle yet ominous voice trickled through the air.

"What! Why?"

"Is she yours?"

Charlemagne hugged me close to him again. "No, the lady belongs to herself."

You were so repulsed earlier. I pouted. *But you don't want to hand me over to the boys, do you?*

"Your words and your actions don't match, Your Majesty," the chancellor commented sarcastically.

"Shut up."

The chancellor flinched and closed his mouth. Then, he glanced over at the frozen Cheryl.

"You're still here?" He tossed the words casually, as though talking to himself, and slowly headed to his tent.

Even as Cheryl trembled, she did not approach us.

Well, that's that, but...

Glenn Masiar.

The child who felt like a sibling to me had been acting strangely. He usually would have done more than just come over by now. It was as if he had forgotten all about us. And I also felt as though I had forgotten about his existence for a moment.

Chills ran down my spine. "Glenn!"

Charlemagne jolted at my shout, and he wasn't the only one.

"Huh?"

"Hmm."

"Oh!"

The spies, who weren't wary of Cheryl and were sitting with their backs turned to her, were also shocked.

I mean, the whole bird situation was surprising, but...

We had all forgotten that Glenn was right there beside us.

Glenn did not answer. He was standing far away and staring at Cheryl. I gathered the fairies and the bird into my arms and called out to him once more.

"Glenn! Get it together!"

"Oh." He finally reacted as though he had recovered his senses. The fairies stopped pinching the bird and turned to face him.

Peep? The blue bird cocked its head again, and its pink

irises sparkled when it saw Glenn.

"Come here," I said nonchalantly. "Are you all right?"

He slowly turned his head to face me. "Sister," he responded. "I remember now. That lady... I know her."

CHAPTER
ONE HUNDRED
AND TWENTY-THREE

"You bitch!" Cheryl's god shouted at her. The god had been awake longer than usual, but she ignored the voice. "That's enough!"

That must be the God of Infatuation. She regarded the god with utter disdain. *Why shouldn't I use as much power as I want when I have it? It's my power now.*

Cheryl already had similar powers as a dark wizard, but now that she had the holy object, she became an even more powerful hypnosis mage. Naturally, she relentlessly used that power for the dark wizards' cause.

The only weakness of the power of hypnosis was that its effectiveness decreased if the person she was trying to hypnotize raised their guard, but...

"Sister."

...if the person was someone she had hypnotized before...

"I remember now. That person. I know her."

...they would find it hard to escape her clutches.

A brief smirk darted across her pale lips and disappeared.

She did not notice Charlemagne watching her.

"You remembered?" asked Scarlett Arman.

Cheryl thought that she was very beautiful in person. Also, she thought it was hilarious that Scarlett was practically in Charlemagne's arms as she held the fairies and a blue bird made of light in her own arms.

To think that I'll be taking her spot soon…

Cheryl was confident that the tyrant would fall in love with her. Confident that she could make him kiss her feet, saturated with lust.

"This woman was my fiancée," Glenn said.

"What?"

The people protecting Charlemagne and Scarlett scoffed, dumbfounded. Cheryl couldn't sense their movements, so she assumed they were Charlemagne's shadowy spies. She wondered if she should hypnotize them as well, but then decided to wait.

"Yes, from when I was young."

"But earlier, you said…"

Glenn Masiar was all she needed to turn the tables.

Emperor Charlemagne lightly wrapped his hand around Scarlett's shoulder. His eyes narrowed at Cheryl, but her gaze was fixed on his hand, so she didn't notice.

Cheryl bit her lip in displeasure. "Now that I think about

it, I remember as well. I heard that I had a fiancé when I was a child. Our engagement was decided before I was even born. I've never seen him before, though."

I changed my face, so let's say we haven't seen each other.

As the thought floated across Cheryl's mind, Glenn paused. Then, he nodded.

"You don't seem curious, Lady Diel," said Charlemagne.

Cheryl turned her head to face him, moving her body in an innocent, delicate manner. "Pardon me, Your Majesty. What is it that you mean?"

"You haven't asked about that child's age."

A trembling voice flowed from her lips. "I have already heard about the young master of the House of Masiar."

To be honest, this type of character wasn't to Cheryl's taste, but she needed to act like this in order to showcase a contrasting type of charm. She caused a breeze to whoosh by again and dizzied his gaze with her thick, swishing red hair.

"So, that's why you weren't surprised to see your fiancé, whom you have never seen before in your life?"

"Yes, Your Majesty. And it is rude to act surprised after meeting someone."

Charlemagne smirked lightly. Even that single smirk flaunted the elegant beauty of the emperor's face.

Cheryl's eyes flashed with emotion.

"Well, then." Charlemagne paused. "Lord Glenn is like a younger brother to Lady Lettie, so you also are Lady Lettie's younger sibling now."

"Yes, I suppose so, Your Majesty."

Something didn't feel right, but she didn't have a reason to reject his efforts to get close to her.

Once I can just get him into the castle... then it will be easy to get close to him in a different sense of the word.

"Oh! In that case, Your Majesty." Cheryl garnished her face with a sensuous smile. "This is also destiny. May I have the pleasure of inviting you to our estate?"

"Surely." A soft smile played on Emperor Charlemagne's lips.

Gorgeous. I want him for myself.

Cheryl deliberately avoided Scarlett's gaze as she smiled brightly. It was the most magnificent smile she could make with this face. Though, she did notice Scarlett's face hardening.

She can't help it, can she?

Now, Cheryl was the one gaining the emperor's attention.

To think that such a simple provocation worked. Amusing.

"Your Majesty, I shall go on ahead and inform the lord of the house that you are on your way."

"Go on, then." The emperor chuckled. He appeared to

have completely let down his guard.

Cheryl had unwavering faith in her powers, so she took the emperor's unexpected change of heart at face value.

Finally, my powers are working.

Then again, this was to be expected. She had the power of a holy object on top of her own powers as a dark wizard.

Not even a Kalior will be able to withstand this combination.

Cheryl quickly recovered her injured pride. "Then I shall take my leave, Your Majesty."

"I'll look forward to it."

"Of course, Your Majesty."

Cheryl slipped back to her estate, blending in as if she were just a regular person.

I couldn't hold back my gloomy feelings as I watched her leave. When I glanced at Charlemagne, I saw him fixated on her receding figure, looking interested. He did not meet my eyes. He wasn't angry, so this probably meant...

He's totally captivated.

That had to be it.

Why, though? She's not his type. I'm closer to his ideal type! How is he so captivated by someone who is the opposite of what he desires? Then again, love overcomes everything.

I may have only learned about romantic relationships through reading, but even I knew that fact. I recalled the emperor's monologue from his first meeting with Cheryl in the novel. He said that it felt like the focus of his life had immediately shifted to her. If the experience was as intense as it was written...

The hand that held my shoulder was as tender as ever, but from my point of view, it was merely kindness toward his dear friend.

Charlemagne was reckless when he was in love.

"Now I know for sure," I muttered dejectedly.

"Lady Scarlett?"

"Yes, Your Majesty?" Replying a bit too late, I hugged the fairies and the bird closer to my chest.

Peep?

"Lettie! Ehehe!"

"Kyahaha! I like this!"

"Mmm!"

The bird and the boys were ecstatic.

Ugh. This sucks, I thought, refusing to meet Charlemagne's eyes. This was clearly jealousy, and it felt like something was gnawing away at my insides.

Hopeless love is tougher than I imagined. I should try my best to not cause any trouble.

I sighed deeply and resolved to get over my feelings as fast as I could. We had to figure out what was so suspicious about her, but that was unrelated to this, so I shouldn't provoke an emperor who was crazy about love.

I felt as though I had reverted back to when I first woke up in Scarlett Arman's body. Hiding my sadness, I turned to Charlemagne. "What are you doing? You should get ready to leave."

"Are you going to ask me why I did what I did?"

"Why should I? You should do what you want, Your Majesty."

"Wait—"

"The lady said she would be waiting. Come on, hurry up. You need to clean your tent and everything."

"Hmm." Charlemagne gave me an odd look. "I don't have anything to do."

"Yeah, well, neither do I."

"We'll take care of everything!" the spies, who had been trying hard to read the room, replied hastily, and vanished.

As I watched them disappear, I tossed Charlemagne a question. "So, how was she?"

Okay then. I'm still a friend. That hasn't changed yet! I mean, love isn't the only thing in this world.

I'll just give up.

I promised myself I would act as bright and bubbly as I could.

"Hmm?"

"Lady Diel, Your Majesty."

He tilted his head.

Why was he pretending he wasn't interested? He fell in love with her at first sight. It was written all over his face. I'd seen it all.

"You know," I said with a titter as I poked his arm. "Promise you'll tell me if you find someone you like, okay?"

"Why? Are you going to kill her?"

Wow, I'm not you. Why would I kill anyone? I smiled meaningfully at him. "Obviously because then I'll have to break off the engagement for y—"

"Lady Scarlett." All traces of laughter had disappeared from his face.

When I saw his burning gaze, I couldn't say anything, but I wanted to give him advice on his future relationship, considering we were friends.

If Cheryl Diel was a dark wizard, that would mean more trouble. *We'd have to knock her out and smuggle her away from that whole operation or take some other action.*

If not that, then I could probably help her with my holy object. That was why I'd mentioned it, but Charlemagne was acting strangely.

He gazed at me for a while before he chuckled huskily. Then he said, in a lower voice than usual, "Don't make jokes like that." The hand that brushed away a strand of hair on my cheek was intimate. "How are you going to handle it if I go insane?"

CHAPTER
ONE HUNDRED AND TWENTY-FOUR

I stared dazedly at Charlemagne. *Why would you go insane? And then...*

Smack! The hearty sound reverberated through the air.

Peep! The pink-eyed bird that had been resting peacefully in my arms cried out. Gill, Nell, and Bell were also gawking at me, their eyes wide open. Charlemagne was looking at me peculiarly with a slight frown.

He stared at me wordlessly and then examined the cheek that I had slapped. His face was even closer now. The lips that had just said that he would go insane were unbelievably well put together, exquisite. All I could see were those lips.

You psycho. This is problematic!

My mind kept tumbling over strange thoughts.

I mean, why did he respond with "I'll go insane" when I told him I would break off the engagement for him? He'll go insane if I break it off? What the hell is he saying?

He had been staring so intently at her earlier. But now that I thought of it, he didn't look like a man in love.

Then why?

If this was a romance novel, I would have screamed, *"It's because he likes you!"*

But this was Charlemagne. I knew how foolhardy he was when he was in love.

But a part of me kept telling me I was wrong.

"Lady Lettie?" he said in a strangled voice, gazing at me.

My eyes were still unwittingly on his lips. I raised my hand toward my face again, but the moment I was about to strike, he grasped it.

"Enough."

I blinked and lifted my eyes to his, and he let out a scoff.

"Lady Lettie, why in the world are you slapping your own cheek?"

At his words, I started to get emotional. *I was being careful not to mess up! But it won't work! I can't do this anymore. I need to ask.*

"That's my line. Why would Your Majesty go insane if I broke off our engagement?"

"Because I like you." The words flew out of his mouth without hesitation, but they weren't lighthearted.

Calm down. He didn't say "love," he said "like."

My lips wouldn't part, however, so I simply looked at him, at a loss.

The hand that he was grabbing twitched. I needed to pull myself together, but he was holding on to my hand.

"It's because I like you, Scarlett."

The way he called me by name and not some silly nickname was satisfying to hear, but I was even more troubled because of it.

Charlemagne loosened the grip he had on my twitching hand, then firmly interlaced his fingers with mine. "Now, it's your turn."

As I stared into his violet eyes, I understood. *I can't avoid this.*

"Why do you keep harming yourself?"

"I-it's not that I'm harming myself, but more like..."

"More like?"

"I'm trying to get ahold of myself, Your Majesty."

He blinked once, seeming taken aback. "There's a reason you need to pull yourself together in relation to me, correct?" The corners of his lips curled upward. "I wonder what that might be?"

You... you...! His exceptionally composed demeanor was infuriating. *Jeez, this is frustrating!*

I had been trying so hard to be cautious with him, unlike my usual self. Ever since I realized my feelings for him, it had been difficult for me to act crazy, like his ideal type.

If anyone else had heard what was going on in my mind, they would have disagreed wholeheartedly, but I didn't know that.

Nothing will happen if I leave things the way they are! Think logically.

Cheryl Diel was already completely different from the one in the novel. There was something suspicious about her, and Charlemagne knew it. Their first meeting had already changed.

Of course, I had no way of knowing other people's deepest thoughts, but Charlemagne hadn't acted the same as he did in the novel when he met Cheryl Diel.

All right, then.

I decided to go for it.

I whispered to the bird and the fairies as calmly as I could, "Hey, can you guys go wait with the chancellor?"

"The chancellor?"

"Clover. The one with the green hair."

The fairies pouted, but when I whispered that I would be right behind them, they giggled and then nodded. They grabbed handfuls of what seemed like the blue bird's feathers and fluttered toward the chancellor's tent. The bird flapped around and smacked their tiny hands away so it could fly to the chancellor on its own.

I opened my mouth to speak to the man who had silently waited for me. "Your Majesty, you keep…"

"Mm-hmm."

"…keep on doing things that make me get the wrong impression. I was trying hard not to misunderstand your cues."

He looked confused. "The wrong impression?"

"Yes. You keep acting like you have feelings for me. Just to be sure, Your Majesty, you don't act like that toward anyone else, do you?" *You better not.*

He blinked rapidly. He looked up at the sky before he turned back to me. "What exactly do you mean by 'acting like that'?"

"Like, bringing your face close to someone and telling them you like them."

He said nothing.

"Or, you know, telling them to take you with them everywhere, or that you'll be by their side…"

His expression became more and more inscrutable, and my initial courage began dissipating as I mumbled on. "But then, your ideal type is the total opposite of me."

"What?" Charlemagne asked, bemused.

I raised my voice a bit louder and kept talking. "I mean, there are some things that apply to me, but I'm not that crazy."

"Craz—"

"Your Majesty. As you've probably already noticed, I'm a simple lady."

His mouth opened a little. He was probably shocked by the sudden flood of words. I was blabbing about things he hadn't even asked about, after all.

But I have so many feelings built up inside me, you know?

I'd settle this once and for all. Cheryl was at the Diel estate, so I had to bring this matter to a close before we went there.

"There's nothing special about me. Well, I am exceptionally pretty, but that's it. Anyway, I don't like standing out, I'm fairly well-behaved, and unlike you, I have a lot of common sense." The more I talked, the more I felt like I was getting further and further away from his ideal woman, and that was depressing. "So, what I'm saying is that... there's no way that Your Majesty would l-love... me."

I fumbled over the word "love," mumbling it as much as possible, yet my cheeks became hot.

Charlemagne was gazing at me with an indecipherable expression. I couldn't tell how he felt, but I was disappointed that he did not agree or disagree with my words.

I went on, a little sulkily, "But if you keep acting like you're interested in me, it's sort of tough on me. That's what

I'm saying." His mouth moved slightly, as though he was about to speak, so I quickly continued. "Basically, you can't say anything if I do start to like you. I even slapped myself to try to get my head on straight, so you can't blame me for it!"

"But, why do you have to try?" he asked.

Jeez! Haven't you been listening?

"I told you. I'm not Your Majesty's type, so I already know that there's no way you'd like me."

"Not that." He shook his head, looking like he had so much he wanted to say.

"Not that?" I looked up at him, confused.

"My god." He brought his hand to his mouth for a moment and then asked me again, "Why did you have to try slapping yourself instead of just asking to break off the engagement?"

I paused.

"You wanted an annulment, didn't you?" he asked.

"You knew about that?"

"Yes."

How? But before I could ask, he continued, "Why didn't you just say you would break it off? It's as if..."

I couldn't speak.

"...you're trying to stop yourself from falling for me."

"H-huh?"

That makes sense…? In other words, I was already falling for him, so I'd tried to stop myself from falling even harder…

"Scarlett." He brought the hand he was still holding to his lips and kissed it softly. As his lips touched my fingertips and his voice murmured my name, the small of my back tingled.

I stared at him, shocked. He'd put it bluntly.

He's asking if I like him.

He likes me in that way.

Images of his darkened irises and all his obsessive reactions filled my mind.

"Yes. You're right."

"I am?"

"Yes."

"You slapped your own cheek because you have feelings for me?"

"That's right…"

"Aha." He grinned. "Well, then. You don't need to slap yourself anymore."

"Wh-why?"

"I like you, Scarlett."

I squeezed my eyes shut and opened them again.

This wasn't a dream.

CHAPTER
ONE HUNDRED AND TWENTY-FIVE

I closed my mouth as I felt my heart pound.

After a short pause, I replied, "M-me too."

He tightened his grip on my hand, just enough so that it wouldn't hurt.

"I like you, Your Majesty."

A gratified smile was on his lips.

"I like you, Your Majesty."

At the other end of the communication bead, Isar's mouth hung open. He was already trying to keep it together after seeing real, live fairies.

Still, thanks to those fairies flying over to Scarlett with the bead, he had been able to talk... no, he *would* have been able to talk to her, but...

"Wow."

A smirk formed on his lips. Astonished, Isar stared at the communication bead. He was watching a scene from his little sister's love life from the best seats in the house.

Or rather, eavesdropping. Scarlett was tightly gripping the communication bead in the hand that Charlemagne wasn't holding.

I can't even hang up right now. I haven't talked to her yet.

Isar assumed that Scarlett's party had arrived just outside the Diel territory, and he wouldn't get the opportunity to tell them his suspicions if he didn't do it now.

But...

"Hehe. Your Majesty."

"Hmm?"

"Then, today's our first day, isn't it?"

"First day?"

"Don't pretend you don't know."

Scarlett's finger poked Charlemagne's side. Based on the location of the communication bead, Isar could see it clearly.

She shoved that finger into his side hard. I bet it hurt.

Charlemagne, however, didn't budge, as though he didn't even feel it. But whether he flinched or not wasn't important. The important thing was the fact that his little sister had jabbed at the tyrant's ribs.

Isar's eyes shook violently. *Does she* want *to die? Even if they're close! That's how she acts toward the emperor?*

"What are you talking about?"

"...ing..."

"Hmm?"

"It's the first day we're dating!"

"Ah."

But in contrast to Isar's expectations, Charlemagne's voice was practically dripping with sweetness.

"I think we have a more solid relationship than just dating."

"We do? Mehehe... More...?" Scarlett's giggle went on for a while.

Isar was flabbergasted. *He thinks Scarlett is endearing even with that laugh...? I would have told her I was talking in my sleep and stampeded out of—*

"You're my fiancée, not just a girlfriend."

Wow. With the way he was talking, he was probably looking at her all sweetly, too. Isar smirked again without even realizing it, but his peace lasted only for a moment.

"Hehe, you're right. Then..."

Mwah.

"Argh!" Isar reacted instinctively to the small smooching sound. "Gross! Did she just..."

Aren't they outside right now? Is she crazy? She kissed the emperor outside... and in broad daylight? Why is she so assertive?

Do it somewhere I can't see!

"Hey!"

Not that there was anything wrong with what was happening, but he didn't want to hear it.

"Hey! Scarlett! Over here! Listen! Scarlett?" After flailing his body around for a moment, Isar hastily called out to Scarlett. "I'm right here!"

She wasn't holding the communication bead high enough, so the only thing she could hear was a faint buzzing sound. Isar shouted even louder, hollering to make his presence known.

Of course, his efforts were futile.

Charlemagne was silent.

Or frozen, to be more precise.

He blinked slowly as he gazed at the lips that had swiftly touched his and parted.

Scarlett's... lips...

He paused for a moment, then his lips wordlessly landed on Scarlett's. His warm, soft lips were sweet, and Scarlett instinctively returned the act.

The tentative movements deepened. Embracing the back of her neck and back with his hands so she couldn't escape,

Charlemagne tasted her obsessively. With soft moans that escaped unconsciously, their kiss deepened even further.

"Arrrgh! Damn it!"

Craaash!

The pitiful clamor of Isar screaming and running away from the communication bead became the background music to their first kiss.

A string of victims to their public display of affection appeared one after the other.

The spies and the chancellor had just finished preparing to leave for the Diel lands when they became speechless at the sight of Charlemagne and Scarlett entwined.

"Ooh…"

"Eek! Oh my god!"

They were now way past their first kiss. They kissed again and again.

They gazed into each other's eyes and murmured a few words, and then kissed again and again.

"Damn!" the chancellor said as he whipped his head away from them. He was looking for the communication bead because he desperately needed something to distract him, but he couldn't find it anywhere.

"Dear fairies, do you know where the communication bead is?"

"I dunnooo!"

"I dooo!"

"Me too!"

"Where is it? Do you know who contacted us?" The chancellor's voice was weepy. He really did not want to see a lovey-dovey couple right now. *Damn! Damn it!*

Bell smiled happily as he watched the miserable chancellor, and then pointed his tiny finger. "Over there! I left it there!"

"It was a boy with black hair!"

"Black hair? Is it Lord Isar? Then..."

The chancellor followed the direction of the finger, and his face went blank. He could see Scarlett holding on tightly to the communication bead.

Oh no...

The three spies, who were covering their faces with both hands and peeping out from between their fingers, regarded the chancellor pityingly.

"Chancellor," No. 1 said. "It might be an emergency pertaining to the empire, so you should retrieve the bead." His voice was grave and quite different from his usual tone, but the chancellor knew that cursed spy was teasing him.

"He's right," No. 3 chimed in, sounding worried. "What if it's something crucial? Come on, Chancellor, please get the bead."

No. 2 went even further. "We'd be forever grateful if you could also tell them that we should get moving, too."

Life sucks.

The chancellor stared at the spies, looking as though he hadn't slept for days. The way their lips were pursed tightly to keep themselves from laughing was the pinnacle of odiousness, but...

Someone had to do it.

"See you back here... alive!" No. 3 waved her hand playfully and said goodbye as he trudged away. She was practically bidding farewell to his life. There was no way that Charlemagne would let anyone live if they interfered now.

Of course, he was the chancellor, so perhaps he wouldn't die.

"Your Majesty..." The chancellor interrupted the couple's sweet moment with a limp voice as the two broke apart.

Not long after that, the party headed over to the Diel territory. And sure enough, Charlemagne's "you won't get away with this" glare was directed wholly at the chancellor.

He's so freaking good at kissing! Not that I have anyone else to compare it to, since I've been single all my life.

Saturated with euphoria and grinning like an idiot, I stepped into the Diel lands.

Peep!

The blue bird had flapped around us raucously until each of the fairies hit it in turn, and then it disappeared. Before it left, it dropped a flower on each of our heads, and we placed them safely in our pockets even as we were moving.

Charlemagne said Baba sent that bird. My mysterious and secretive friend must have sent us something that would help.

And he had. The thick mist that had fallen over the entire land up to the gates of the estate couldn't come near us.

They said the fog was poisonous, right?

The fairies had been elated after chasing the blue bird away. They'd chattered on about things I didn't even ask about, and among those things was information about that mist. They also talked about the effects of the flowers we were holding, although they would only last for a few days.

Baba was truly a reliable friend.

Now, onto other things...

I glanced at Charlemagne. Our eyes met, as though he had been looking at me as well. I wriggled the hand that was holding his, and a soft smile formed on his lips.

I must be nuts. I'm so happy. I can't believe we had our first make-out session right after a little kiss!

"Welcome, Your Majesty, and your company as well," Cheryl Diel said, interrupting my thoughts.

Even as Cheryl Diel stood in front of me, her hair swishing in the breeze again, I merely smiled.

I'm invincible right now! I felt like I could do anything. *So, I hope you show me as many things as you can.*

"Lady Arman?"

"Lady Diel, thank you for inviting us."

I was looking forward to our stay.

CHAPTER
ONE HUNDRED AND TWENTY-SIX

Cheryl Diel embodies the color red.

That was how she was described in the novel. But the only thing I remembered while I was watching the videos was her red hair. She was beautiful, but the color of her hair had left the strongest impression. But now that I was looking at her again, something else captured my attention—her eyes.

I glanced at Glenn, who looked gaunt. "You said you knew Glenn."

"We knew each other briefly when we were young," Cheryl answered.

"When you were young, huh?"

Her green eyes flashed. It was only for a moment, but they flashed like those of an evil character in a comic. The color of her eyes was a clear and brilliant green, but they somehow felt cloudy, like a dead person's eyes.

Maybe it's related to something. Maybe she is a dark wizard. Well, that would change the genre of the novel from romance to horror.

I shuddered at the sudden thought, completely horrified. Charlemagne stepped closer, almost hugging me.

This man! Why is he doing everything right?

Trying to hide my stupid grin, I turned around and
pretended to look at Charlemagne, but I was really glancing
at Glenn behind us.

"Hmm." The way he was staring vacantly ahead when we
were talking about a subject he would have chimed in about
was unsettling. He hadn't been like that when it was just us.

*Cheryl must have done something to him, right? But how
is her influence over him so strong? He seems like a completely
different person.*

I didn't have time to interrogate him again. It would
have been meaningless anyway. The circumstances were
crystal clear even without an interrogation.

It's hypnosis.

Charlemagne had spoken to everyone except Glenn
before we entered the estate. *"There's a high chance that she is
a dark wizard."*

He had then asked me how I felt about going back to the
capital, and of course, I refused. *"There's no guarantee that I'll
be safe even if I do go back. I'm going to stay by your side. Not to
mention, I'll probably be of help, too."*

I had good reason for saying that. I had heard a surprising

truth when I visited the elders before leaving on this journey. They said my mother was a distant relative of the Rashahel family, so it seemed that the lucky experiences we had during our time inside the book weren't just luck. The elders didn't know the exact details, but Scarlett Arman's mother was connected to the Rashahels in some way.

Maybe she was from a branch family? Or perhaps... based on the video I saw that time I discovered Scarlett's secret diary...

That was when I had realized that Scarlett was not Baron's daughter, but the former duke, Aaron's daughter instead. The dying woman from that video certainly hadn't been ordinary.

There's a high chance that she could have used magic, considering she said weird things to Scarlett, like how she was a halfling or whatever. So maybe...

Maybe her blood had been far more saturated with Rashahel blood than the elders knew. That was also possibly why I was so unusually fortunate.

"Charl, that basically means that I'm a lucky charm! I'll be of help even if I stay still and don't do anything."

Lightly admonishing the chancellor, whose eyes were shining inquisitively, Charlemagne had nodded.

On a side note, we had decided on new nicknames for each other: Charl and Lett.

"*I didn't say anything because it wasn't necessary, Lett, but I have good instincts.*"

"*Instincts?*"

"*About dark wizards.*" He'd lifted the corners of his lips menacingly. "*It didn't apply to the Temple, but we'll see how it works here. I notice those things instinctively.*"

According to his words, his intuition had played a vital role in his extermination of dark wizards. Almost all the issues that had labeled him a tyrant to the rest of the world were connected to dark wizards in some way.

Wow. All that with just a gut feeling?

"*And you've never been wrong before, not once?*"

"*Yes.*"

Swaggering, the chancellor had piped up, "*He has dealt with a demon hidden among humans before, which we only found out about once it was killed. My god! I couldn't believe it at first, either. Our Majesty is virtually the nemesis of the dark wizards.*"

There was nothing to do but believe him.

"*It's even more so when I'm together with this sword.*"

He was referring to the black sword he bore at his side even now. When Charl saw me looking at it, he told me to focus on him as he kissed me again.

And after that, we arrived at the estate.

Ah! I'm smiling again! This is why people date, isn't it?

"Ahem, ahem."

When I cleared my throat, Charl cocked his head a little. Seeing the small smile play around his lips, I could tell he knew what I was thinking about. Hiding my embarrassment, I shifted my eyes to No. 3, who had been standing by Glenn to keep an eye on him. Charl had acted almost pleased when Glenn had acted strangely because of the hypnosis, but now he was lifting an eyebrow in disapproval.

Goodness.

Anyway, No. 3 now looked like a regular noble lady. *I think she said her name was Samiah Ester.* She also said it was one of her many identities. Samiah Ester was supposedly a lady who rarely left the house due to her frail body.

It's so interesting that she insisted on dressing up as a lady while here, especially as a lady who had suddenly joined our party.

She didn't look like a regular noble lady, though.

Glenn was struggling to catch a glimpse of Cheryl as he staggered and stumbled around, since we were hiding her from his view. No. 3 was holding on to him tightly, glaring at him with her eyes. It was menacing.

I think it would be best if you took him inside first. I signaled to her with my eyes, and No. 3 blinked surreptitiously. She understood.

Whack!

"Oh, my! Lord Glenn!"

At the speed of light, No. 3 had smacked the back of Glenn's neck. He crumpled without a sound, and No. 1 propped him up. Turning down the corners of his mouth to stop himself from laughing, No. 1 took the unconscious Glenn to the back of the procession.

No. 3 turned to Cheryl, who was staring in their direction. "It looks like Lord Masiar is not feeling well today. It seems we must acquaint ourselves later, Lady Diel."

"I see. But... who are you?"

"Please call me Lady Samiah Ester."

"Yes, Lady Ester. What might your relationship with that lord be?" Not showing any interest in the man who used to be her fiancé, Cheryl spoke only to No. 3.

That lord? Then again, she's probably flustered at the sudden appearance of some lady she doesn't know.

No. 3 gave an innocent smile. "You did not know? Lord Glenn and I are friends," she lied nonchalantly.

"I have not heard him mention you before."

"Well, you did say you only knew him when you were young, did you not?"

And if that's supposedly true, you can't say anything even if you don't know about No. 3!

Cheryl pursed her lips, her doe-like daintiness disappearing and a humorless expression taking its place. She briefly observed No. 3 before smiling again and nodding.

"Yes, perhaps that is so. Allow me to show you somewhere he can rest."

"Thank you kindly."

No. 3 was going to take this opportunity to leave the estate with Glenn and monitor it from afar. No. 2, who had been standing stoically and pretending to be a knight, followed behind No. 3.

"Now then, Your Majesty. Please come this way. I have specially prepared the best room in the mansion for you."

Cheryl smiled coyly at Charlemagne, but he did not answer, let alone look at her. More precisely, it seemed that he hadn't heard her at all. He was wordlessly staring at my lips with an intense look in his eyes.

I swallowed back the laughter that was threatening to spill out and gently punched him. "Your Majesty! The lady is speaking to you."

It really was a gentle punch.

"Lett? Are you mad at m—"

"You must answer her!"

"Lead us," he said to Cheryl.

At Charlemagne's chilling voice, Cheryl stiffly turned

around, her smile still frozen in place, and she led the way.

You didn't even answer because you knew he wouldn't hear that, either. I watched her back pityingly as we followed her steps.

The chancellor whispered from behind, "Lady Scarlett. Would you at least try not to smile?"

"Ahem."

And just like that, we entered the castle without catching a glimpse of the lord who ruled it.

Later that evening...

Glenn Masiar was found dying.

CHAPTER
ONE HUNDRED AND TWENTY-SEVEN

About five hours earlier. . .

"I have prepared rooms for Lady Arman, the chancellor, and the other guest in a different part of the mansion."

Cheryl sounded quite cold. Anyone would think of her a regular noble lady who was hostile to the emperor's fiancée because of her interest in the emperor.

I wouldn't need to be so on edge if that was all there was to her.

I smiled brightly. "I see. Please show us to our rooms."

I hesitated briefly, wondering if I should say that I wanted to stay with Charlemagne. However, our goal was to find something suspicious about Cheryl, so I decided to meekly do as she said for now.

Cheryl took the lead, and I was about to follow her, but my body didn't move forward even as I walked.

"Your Majesty?"

"Charl."

"Yes, Charl. You need to let go of me so I can go."

"Go where?"

I tried to send him a message with my eyes, but the "let's talk with our eyes" thing was a lot more difficult in real life.

"We're engaged, so there's no need for us to be apart. Lead the others, Lady Diel." The soft smile he held for me was as sweet as honey, but his voice was as chilling as the winter wind.

Oh my, he wants to be with me!

I frowned to keep the corners of my lips from sneaking up at the sudden thought.

Trying my best to ignore the chancellor and No. 1, who was posing as an attendant, as they stared at us with cold, dead eyes, I arranged my face to look prim. I stepped closer to Charlemagne.

Cheryl's voice shook, "We haven't prepared anything for Lady Arman in that room—"

"Then, you should hurry up." Charlemagne cut her off as he pulled me to his side. "I imagine it won't take long. Right, Lady Diel?"

"Of course, Your Majesty," Cheryl replied reluctantly. I surreptitiously observed her actions.

Yeah, something's off. Let's consider the worst-case scenario: what if she's a dark wizard, and a high-ranking one at that, who kidnapped Glenn?

There's no way she would be so lame.

I mean, I could see right through her. And that wasn't all. I'd been getting a weirdly familiar feeling since we stepped foot in the estate. It was very faint, which was why I originally agreed to go to the room Cheryl prepared for me.

But there was no reason for me to put myself in danger on purpose. Plus, Charlemagne didn't want me to leave him. I gently held his hand and prepared to open the door to "the specially prepared best room."

"Oh, Lady Diel!" I shouted towards Cheryl, as she, the chancellor and No. 1 started walking away. "Those two guests are incredibly close as well, so please put them both in one room."

It'll be safer if No. 1 and the chancellor share a room, since the chancellor can't fight that well, right?

The three people in front halted sharply and turned around.

"Lady Arman! What in the world are you talking about?"

"M-me, incredibly close with this beanpole? Bleurgh!"

Should I have said they are besties? Doesn't that sound kind of childish, though?

Once again hoping to relay my feelings through my eyes, I stared meaningfully at the two of them. "You are! So extremely close."

The chancellor and No. 1 both grabbed the backs of their necks in the same pose.

See? They're besties. They looked chummy, like little boys who fought and argued. But what was wrong with them? Why couldn't they understand I was trying to keep them safe by putting them together?

Charlemagne gazed intently at me.

"What? They are."

"They are."

Am I imagining things? He looked like he was trying hard not to laugh.

I grinned at him. "You're happy with everything I say, even if it's gibberish, right?"

"Hmm?"

"I understand. I'm like that, too. Ah, is this why people have romantic relationships?"

I turned back to Cheryl. "Anyway! You heard me, Lady Diel. I'm counting on you."

Cheryl surveyed the chancellor and No. 1 with an odd look and then nodded. She didn't seem to be in the right mind to answer. I studied her carefully and then went inside the room with Charlemagne. The door closed with a clack.

"Charl, we need to find out if there's anything strange before..."

I turned to face him as I whispered, but he was standing closer to me than I had expected, and his expression was strange.

"...dinner time."

He tilted his head as he silently asked me how I felt about what he was going to do.

Communicating with your eyes works in these types of situations as well.

The trivial thought crossed my mind as I lifted my chin in response to his question. He pressed his lips against mine as though he wanted to consume me.

In the middle of the enemy's territory.

Lettie is smooching again, the fairies said to each other.

They didn't have to speak out loud to communicate with each other. Not only that, but their conversations were also unconstrained by time. The three fairies could use that power instinctively, but they didn't have any older fairies to explain exactly what kind of phenomenon it was, so they didn't understand it in detail.

It wasn't as though the eggplant fairies would have told the three babies about it, and they wouldn't have been able to anyway. The eggplant fairies didn't know about the power because they couldn't escape the constraints of time, either.

Kiss, kiss. I know even if I can't hear, Gill muttered sullenly as he plugged his ears.

Nell shook his head. *It's not chu, chu. It's choo—choo—*

Yep. Choo—choo—

Lettie said not to say that! Bell shouted energetically.

Then, what do we call it? Nell tipped his head to the side.

She told us not to listen at all! Bell answered, still enthusiastic.

The truth was that she had told them to go somewhere else, and Bell wasn't the only one who had heard her request.

Do we have to keep plugging our ears, then?

Yep! That's what she said! Bell answered Gill's doleful question with the same energy as before. Bell was delighted right now, and Gill and Nell felt the same.

Because Lettie is happy!

Lettie was especially happy when she was with that silver-haired human. Her heart, mind and soul glowed with a soft, fluffy light.

Had the fairies been older, they would have realized that the feeling was love, but the younglings could only feel it and not understand it. Still, what was good was good.

It *was* good, but...

I hope they finish soon.

Me, too.

I'm bored...

Keeping their ears covered was boring.

They fell silent for a while, until the Fairy of Light, Nell, said: *This place is weird.*

It is! The Fairy of Water, Gill, nodded in agreement. They had sensed something abnormal the moment they entered the Diel lands. An unpleasant flow of mana. Of course, they had noticed other bizarre things as well.

H-he's weird, too.

They were referring to the child of Rashahel, Glenn Masiar. He was a pretty child with white-gold hair and blood-red eyes. Lettie was the best, but his aura wasn't bad either. But right now, they couldn't feel anything from him.

No, more than that...

He feels rotten!

We can't eat rotten fruit. That's why we give it to the earth.

He's not a fruit.

Then, what do we do with rotten men?

The pure voices began discussing something chilling.

We give rotten men to the earth, too, Nell said tenderly.

Gill gasped. *E-even Lettie?*

Lettie is not rotten! She's not rotten! Bell shouted tearfully.

I'm not giving Lettie to the earth even if she is rotten!

Yeah! You're right!

We're not going to let her rot to begin with.

But if you touch rotten things, you rot, too.

Then we'll stop her from touching him!

The timid little Gill let out a sigh of relief at his brothers' determined words. The fairy boys nodded gravely as they spoke one last time.

If the earth doesn't want it, we'll keep it.

Yeah, it might become clean again if we wash and dry it.

Yep! We can do that if it's just the soul. Let's tell Lettie we'll give it to her if she wants it!

Okay!

Cheryl Diel smiled coldly as she made up her mind.

Glenn Masiar. The fact that the others were trying very hard to protect him meant that he had become an important part of their group.

I wondered how much I could use him since it hadn't been long since they last met each other, but...

This was favorable to her. She thought about the chancellor and the spies who had deviously gotten under her skin, as well as the tyrant who hadn't reacted to her in the least, and...

Scarlett Arman.

Right after her God of Infatuation had fallen asleep, Cheryl started feeling something unpleasant about Scarlett again, like she was stabbing her through the heart.

I can't afford to waste time.

Her initial wish to go along with the situation had vanished. She could not understand what had happened, as it occurred without warning.

What does my god falling asleep have to do with that wench?

She couldn't understand what had happened. What Cheryl didn't realize was that the day the tyrant had cut off one of her arms, Scarlett had unknowingly planted some of her sacred power inside her.

In order to end this strange situation, Cheryl decided to kill Glenn Masiar sooner than she had initially planned.

He was to be a sacrifice anyway, so I'll recover the sacrifice before I deal with her.

They seemed to care deeply for Scarlett, so she would make a good pawn. With that thought in mind, Cheryl leisurely headed toward the banquet hall.

It was time for the dinner banquet.

ONE HUNDRED AND TWENTY-EIGHT

Peep! Peeeep!

The blue bird familiar told Baba what had happened with Scarlett.

"Hmm. It's all happening too fast."

Things were progressing far quicker than Baba had expected. He expected that Scarlett and Charlemagne would encounter a dark wizard, but he hadn't imagined they would walk right into the Diel territory, which was connected to the dark wizards' base of operations.

Baba wiped away his cold sweat. "Well, the place is probably empty right now."

They might be lucky as the head of the dark wizards most likely wouldn't be there.

"Nothing dangerous will happen... probably."

That traveling party would be able to handle everything if the leader wasn't there, since they had the emperor, Scarlett, and those skillful spies.

I still don't know why that chancellor is there, though. But I doubt he'll die.

The problem was Glenn Masiar.

Baba gazed deeper into the blue bird's eyes, which recorded everything it had seen. He saw Glenn attacking the third spy while the dinner banquet was being held and then saw him slip out of the mansion to stand in the middle of the garden.

Baba had never talked to him personally, but he knew who Glenn was. He was someone who qualified as a sacrifice.

Though he's not as good a sacrifice as the Arman siblings.

Scarlett, as well as that bad-tempered Isar Arman, would be high-quality sacrifices for the dark wizards. Neither Isar nor the current duchess knew this, but Rashahel blood flowed in the duchess' veins, too. The instincts and intuitions that she trusted so much originated from that faint trace of Rashahel blood.

Perhaps she's from a branch of the branch family.

The siblings would have felt the pull of their blood sooner or later. They wouldn't have stood by and watched each other die, no matter how much bad blood there was between them. If things had played out according to destiny, Isar would have lunged at the dark wizards to prevent Scarlett's death. Even if he failed and died.

Well, all of that is meaningless now.

"It appears their situation isn't too bad right now."

Though to make sure, Baba decided to summon another familiar to watch the capital. The Temple's movements were suspicious, but none of them were directly targeting Isar at the moment. He was protected by the power around the Arman estate, and he was always with Charlemagne's people at the palace.

But Glenn Masiar...

When Baba spoke after a long silence, his voice was cold. "He will die."

That child had separated from the others in the heartland of the dark wizards. Not only that, but he was also afflicted by black magic. This wasn't the first time it happened either, so even the luck of Rashahel wouldn't be able to save him now.

"It's a shame, but..."

There was nothing Baba could do to save him, so he gave up. But he was confused.

"Why is the dark wizard trying to kill him?"

No dark wizard would think to kill a Rashahel unless they were completely stupid.

Kalior, Arman, and Rashahel.

The way to harness the power of these three houses was simple: Destroy them all at once or kill the one who was born with the strongest power. The power of the three dead gods could not flow from the strongest to weakest, which meant it was impossible for a weak vessel to absorb formidable powers.

If an entire house was massacred at the same time, those fragments of power would gather into an appropriate vessel who was closest to the physical location of the house. If the most powerful one was killed, all the power would flow into an appropriate vessel outside of the house instead. In such an instance, the other two houses wouldn't inherit the power.

The dark wizards had massacred the House of Rashahel using the first method, and Emperor Kalior had attempted to absorb the power with the second one. The first method applied to their current circumstance.

In other words, if the weak Rashahel child was killed, his power would first go to a powerful member of the house. But if Glenn Masiar died now, his power wouldn't flow into a dark wizard but into Scarlett Arman.

It'll only be a good thing for Scarlett.

Of course, there was nothing good about anyone dying, but he was thinking from a dark wizard's point of view. If the dark wizards were in their right mind, they wouldn't kill him there.

Baba hesitated.

Don't they know that Scarlett also has Rashahel blood? No, that can't be. The dark wizards would have found out through their investigations by now, especially with how strong their leader was.

If the Diel wizard doesn't know... "Is she a throwaway pawn?"

The dark wizard in the Diel territory might just being used.

Baba's eyes narrowed before a faint sigh escaped his lips. It didn't make sense they would sacrifice one of their few remaining dark wizards. In that case, would it be better to view this as a mistake they were making because of the luck of Rashahel?

"If that's the case, then it's good for us, right?"

His god didn't reply, having become sulky. In the distant past, his god didn't have the best relationship with the Rashahels.

Though he's working for the dead gods right now.

Baba's face was reflected clearly on the surface of the Mirror Lake. It was different from what he looked like now—it was his real form from long ago.

His long pink hair fluttered in the wind, and a mysterious smile bloomed on the lips of the reflection in the Mirror.

It was like the petals of twilight.

Glenn Masiar felt an intense chill come over him.

He wanted to go somewhere warm. This place was dark and humid. Standing in the middle of the garden that was thick with mist, he searched endlessly for something.

For our god.

Someone kept whispering in his mind.

For the beautiful one.

He had never thought that anything was beautiful aside from himself because he rarely saw anyone more beautiful than him. But upon hearing those words, he didn't think of his sister or that jerk emperor. Instead, he envisioned a face many would consider ugly, yet he found beautiful. His body, which had initially reacted violently in revulsion, eventually calmed down.

You need to die gladly.

"Gladly."

The dark wizard's magic, which had narrowly missed his heart during the first affliction, had now hit its target and turned it black. The only reason it had taken this long was because of the flower that Baba had sent.

Glenn pulled out the dagger he used as his main weapon. The pure white blade glinted sharply.

Shnk. Thud.

His body fell limply onto the ground.

"Charl, I think we should check on Glenn."

"All right. It appears that she's done something to him since she's not bothering us. No. 1, where's No. 3?"

"I can't reach her."

Cheryl Diel had prepared an early dinner banquet to welcome them. Once it was over, Scarlett and Charlemagne's group walked aimlessly toward a desolate area. Along the way, they saw something that caused them to halt their steps in unison.

A small boy lay in a pool of blood in the middle of the decrepit Diel garden.

"Huh? Glenn!" Scarlett recovered her senses first and was running toward Glenn when she grasped her chest.

Boom.

Her heart pounded as though it had been dropped from the top of the sky to the bottom of the earth.

Boom.

An ominous aura began slithering out of Glenn's body as he lay there barely hanging on to life.

Black magic.

Holding Scarlett tightly as she crumpled, Charlemagne glared coldly at the scene before his eyes. "Lett!" he called as he examined her current state. *She hasn't been afflicted by black magic.* He could tell immediately.

Scarlett was clutching at her heart, but the aura that twitched around it wasn't dark or evil. In fact, it was the most powerful, pure glow he had ever seen.

Her body had been thrown into shock, but all the aura flowing inside her was being replaced with a bright glow. This change had happened quite swiftly.

Charlemagne could only think of one thing: *The power that protects the lord of the house.*

The spies stood around Charlemagne, and the chancellor gathered the fairies into his arms. Whether Glenn lived or died wasn't important right now. They had predicted this outcome for Glenn ever since they realized the hypnosis couldn't be fully undone—even with the power of the fairies.

But right now, the most important thing was Scarlett. She was the only one who mattered to Charlemagne.

Through her haze, Scarlett stretched her hand toward Glenn.

Then the fairies, who had been silently watching Glenn, suddenly flew into the air. Light, fire, and water—the purest powers in the world whirled and blended to create a bright, white needle of light.

The moment it touched Glenn's heart, a black spike appeared out of nowhere. The spike, imbibed with a noxious purple mana, silently inched towards Scarlett.

A gust of wind whistled through the air. It was on a completely different level than Cheryl's forced breeze. It was a cold, heavy natural wind—no, it was a storm.

Screeeech!

A scraping noise pierced the air as the rushing black storm whirled to block the spike of mana that was heading straight for Scarlett. And in the eye of the storm, a twisted smile marred Charlemagne's face as he clutched the half-unconscious Scarlett tightly in his arms.

"It seems they underestimated us."

In reaction to Charlemagne's gritted words, the black blade that had been speared through the ground let out an exquisite cry.

CHAPTER
ONE HUNDRED AND TWENTY-NINE

Crash!

The storm quaked loudly as it collided with something outside. Charlemagne waved his arm lightly, but he didn't stop holding onto Scarlett. Her safety was more important to him than anything else.

"Scarlett," he called to her as cold sweat dripped down her forehead.

"...them..." she said in a faint voice. He lowered his ear to her lips to hear it.

You need to capture them.

"Yes, I know." His eyes were icy as he softly stroked her hair. Scarlett's body was stabilizing, but she was too exhausted to do anything at the moment. "Don't worry and get some rest."

Scarlett closed her eyes at his tender touch.

"At your five o'clock, Your Majesty," the chancellor reported, once he and No. 1 had confirmed Scarlett was safe.

"I have gotten in touch with No. 2 and No. 3," said No. 1.

The chancellor had terrible fighting skills, but his instincts were excellent. "This is definitely the work of a dark wizard, even though they've concealed their whereabouts." His hatred for the dark wizards was considerable, even though he didn't show it.

"Is it Cheryl Diel?" Charlemagne asked.

"I don't have any clear evidence, but most likely."

"Do you think Lord Glenn is alive?"

"He's dead."

In the eye of the storm, all three men shared cold looks with each other.

"The fairies looked like they were doing something."

"They can't bring back the dead no matter what they do."

"Hmm..."

The black spike screeched again, and the storm began to lessen.

"No. 1."

"Yes, my liege."

"Protect her." Charlemagne carefully transferred the unconscious Scarlett into No. 1's arms.

The chancellor flopped onto the ground next to them like it was the most natural thing to do. Regardless of how much he hated dark wizards, there wasn't much he could do when it came down to a physical battle like this.

"I don't care if he dies, so focus on protecting Scarlett."

"Yes, of course!"

"Argh! Am I being abandoned?"

Neither of them spared a glance at the groaning chancellor. He let out a small *tsk* and shuffled closer to Scarlett.

Charlemagne gripped his sword tightly, but then his gaze shifted toward the opening that was forming through the storm. No more words were necessary.

With a speed incomparable to anything the aides had ever seen, Charlemagne flew into the air, with his trusted sword, Opere, humming lightly in the background.

With a pure buzz, the black spike that had been trying to pierce Scarlett's heart exploded into thorn-like shards.

"I guess I'm not the target," she said.

Clang!

Charlemagne knew there were more thorns that he couldn't see than ones he could. They zipped endlessly at him, but none of them hit their mark. He blocked every single thorn as he judged the direction of the mana flow.

"The mark of Lycos."

That was the symbol Scarlett had told him about—but he noticed the flow of mana was drawing the mark. It was strange.

The path that mana took inside a person's body was inherent and couldn't be casually changed, but this path was being forced to complete the image of that symbol. He couldn't clearly see who the perpetrator was yet. However...

Are they trying to test me?

Charlemagne noticed that the unknown dark wizard was performing magic with only one hand. He let out a small laugh. They were a highly skilled opponent if they could expel this much power without using both hands.

Opere.

When he called to his sword, it hummed in response as it destroyed every thorn down to its last molecule.

Your prey is over there.

Kyaaagh!

People called his black sword, Opere, the "demon sword." It soon became a symbol of the tyrant. Opere was the last ego sword left in the world, and it was also the mightiest blade.

But unbeknownst to the people, this sword...

"Opere Kalior."

...was also a holy object handed down through the House of Kalior.

The Temple would have flipped on its head if they knew Opere was such a rare treasure. Coincidentally, Opere Kalior was also the name of the sickly young lord of the house who had helped them when they were trapped inside the cursed book.

"So, you succeeded in becoming an actual sword."

Once the flurry of thorns subsided, the sword that had only ever communicated with Charlemagne through sounds suddenly spoke out loud.

– What?

"I've met you before."

– I have no recollection of such a meeting.

"As I thought. It wasn't just a made-up legend."

– What do you mean?

"Don't worry about it. The important thing is that I met you, the young genius who wanted to become a sword. We'll talk later."

Now was not the time for conversation. This much talking was enough to successfully establish communication with his sword.

"Let's destroy that one first."

– Fine! the sword answered gruffly, sounding like a young boy forcing himself to sound tough.

Charlemagne slid his sword toward the dwindling thorns. They stopped in a line that followed his sword's movement, and then flipped around to shoot back in the direction they had come from. Charlemagne glided close behind the flying thorns. And then...

"Ugh!"

He grabbed someone in a black robe by the throat—it was a man.

"Tell me everything you know."

The dark wizard thrashed as Charlemagne's hand circled his throat without hesitation.

"Were you after Scarlett Arman?"

– *It looks like it,* Opere answered, ramming itself into the dark wizard's heart.

"You can read minds?"

– *Only if it's the mind of my prey.*

Charlemagne transferred his gaze back to the dark wizard. "Whose orders?"

– *I can see a red-haired woman.*

"Where is she?"

– *He says she was here not too long ago.*

"So?"

"U-ugh...!"

Controlling the blade so that the dark wizard wouldn't die immediately, Charlemagne's fingers gripped the man's throat even tighter. "Where is she?"

– *He doesn't know.*

Charlemagne stopped talking and started walking around the Diel estate. Opere started sniggering when it read his will.

The next moment, half of the mansion was destroyed.

"She isn't in that half."

– She isn't in this half, either.

"Have you read all of his mind?" Charlemagne glanced at the dark wizard, whose eyes had rolled to the back of his head.

– Of course, Opere replied in an excited boyish voice. *This clown worked for that woman for a long time while he lived here. He has quite a bit of information.*

"Ugh... guh..."

Opere started reading aloud the information that the dark wizard was involuntarily giving away. It wondered how Charlemagne had known what it had been doing all this time. There was one thing he knew for sure—this Kalior was the best out of them all.

– He wasn't a noble in the first place. Also, there is another dark wizard who isn't here. The leader. Well, well. I found something useful.

"Speak."

– This territory is the gateway to the depths. This one doesn't know where the passageway is, though.

"Hmm."

The more Opere spoke, the more Charlemagne's expression changed. Its voice was becoming more and more excited.

– He's seen the three dark wizards gathered in a cave!

Was Opere's personality always like this? Charlemagne thought to himself. The young boy who had helped him in the book had been far sharper and pricklier.

– This one's life is literally flashing before his eyes. Wow, what a boring life he lived. He served the dark wizards because of his ambitions, but all he did his whole life was study.

"Hmm?"

Opere continued blathering on about things Charlemagne didn't even ask for.

– He's full of regret that he never got to enjoy any destruction, annihilation, and whatnot! I can read it all!

"I see."

It seemed that the sword wanted to be praised by him.

– I couldn't leave my bed to take even a few steps because I was sick. He's so ungrateful. Let's kill him.

"I wasn't planning on letting him live to begin with."

Whatever the case, this dark wizard's sad life still held some useful information, even though Charlemagne wasn't interested in learning more.

They soon reached the entrance to the dark wizards'

base of operations. He felt a suspicious energy emanating from the stairs nearby. He stared intently in that direction.

"As expected from the mightiest sword in the world," he said to Opere. "Incredible."

Even when Charlemagne had obliterated the entire House of Pan's Assassins, he hadn't been able to find the entrance. *I only found a lead on the Temple, but Opere found this information so effortlessly.* Charlemagne patted his sword as it prattled on enthusiastically.

A moment later, a hidden door appeared in front of him. It appeared when he shoved the unconscious dark wizard in front of it.

Charlemagne put his hand on the knob, and it turned with a rusty creak.

Something lunged violently at Charlemagne as though it wanted to consume him, but right before the unseen claws could reach him...

"Mmm..."

Charlemagne paused as he could hear Scarlett regaining consciousness back in the garden.

"Lett." Leaving the knocked out dark wizard, Charlemagne put the dark wizard's base, which he had so desperately been searching for, behind him as he ran back to the garden to check on Scarlett.

Crack! Swish! Swish!

The black arm that missed him by inches swiped fruit-lessly at the empty air.

CHAPTER
ONE HUNDRED AND THIRTY

My mind was so clear that it was almost shocking, but that wasn't all. If the fairies had been looking in my direction right now, they would have caused a scene.

They would be able to feel that something has changed.

My line of sight had broadened, and I could feel that my aura had grown stronger.

"Are you all right, Lady Scarlett?" No. 1 asked, his voice full of concern.

I tried to figure out what had happened to me as I looked around. *I think I fainted because my heart pounded too hard.*

I was lying on a piece of navy fabric, and another bundle of fabric was on top of me, protecting me from any dirt.

Why is it so warm? I didn't know where it had come from, but the fabric covered my entire body—only my face peeked out.

Now that I looked at it... it looks like clothes. But I thought I was...

"Charl?"

...in Charlemagne's arms! Where's my boyfriend?

How wonderful would it have been if I could have seen his face the moment I opened my eyes?

No, he couldn't have. Did he leave to capture the dark wizard on his own? He can't.

Charlemagne couldn't have fought against the dark wizards on his own here. We'd have to face them together.

"Lady Scarlett? I couldn't hear you. Are you all right?" the chancellor asked.

I put a bit more force into my voice. "Where is Charl?"

My question was full of concern and anxiety, and my voice shook, not that I intended it to. Both men regarded me with incredibly unfamiliar expressions.

What's wrong with them?

Neither of them ended up answering my question.

"Lett."

"Oh!"

Charlemagne had arrived without my knowledge. I swiftly swept my eyes over him and saw that he wasn't hurt anywhere. Letting out a sigh of relief, I got up immediately.

"Wait, the lady was listless, which was most unlike herself, just a moment ago."

What?

"I-is this the p-power of love?" No. 1 stammered as he

muttered along with the chancellor. I glared at them playfully and then fell into Charlemagne's arms.

"Lett. Are you all right?"

"I'm feeling great."

"Good."

I thought he would have noticed that I didn't collapse because I was attacked, but only because after my answer did his voice relax, and I smiled like an idiot at that.

"Oh, look!"

The three men turned to see what I suddenly pointed my finger at.

"They're safe," Charlemagne murmured. No. 2 and No. 3 were approaching us.

"Tsk, tsk. Are you two all right?" asked the chancellor.

"Yes, sure."

"Yes."

No. 1 wordlessly swept his eyes over the two and then let out a small laugh. The two spies came closer, a little shiftily, and fell to their knees in front of Charlemagne.

"Get up, it's fine," he said before they could say anything, hugging me from behind as he sat down on the cloth on the ground. "There's nothing going on right now, so report. What happened?"

We all huddled around. No. 2 and No. 3 both sighed and

looked around. Their eyes rested on the fallen Glenn and the fairies flying around him. Then, with difficulty, they tore their eyes from him and made their report.

"Everything went smoothly until we arrived at the prepared room with Lord Glenn."

"About seven minutes later, a butler knocked on the door and informed us that he had brought people to serve us before dinner. But then…"

"Lord Glenn started acting strangely after they left." No. 3, who was wearing comfortable clothes instead of being dressed as a noble lady, tilted her head as she recounted the incident.

"He started acting strange?"

"Yes, Lady Arman. It felt like the hypnosis had grown more powerful, but the people who had come in were just regular people."

"If one of them had strengthened the black magic, that can only mean one of two things," Charlemagne said.

No. 2 nodded. "Yes. A dark knight that was used after death, or…"

"A dark wizard powerful enough to avoid detection."

"Either way, it doesn't change the fact that there's a dark wizard who is stronger than any we have encountered up until now."

"What do you mean?" I asked. A powerful dark wizard?

"The dark wizard is probably someone we won't be able to kill on the first try. The fact that they can command dark knights and perfectly hide their identity points to that."

"I see." *Then they're a dark wizard who will die on the second try, right?*

It was kind of ridiculous how non-threatening it felt. I had a feeling that the black magic I'd caught a glimpse of earlier was not really so insignificant.

"Well, I'm glad everyone is safe… except for one person." I looked over at Glenn, worried, and everyone followed suit, but they started talking in a way that was so unaffectionate, even cold.

"He's not dead, then? I thought he'd die. That young lord is very lucky."

"But considering how he was hypnotized so easily—it seems mental strength isn't his forte."

"Eh, it was probably easier since it was his second time. It's like what you said, No. 3. He has a tenacious grip on life."

At the spies' words, I asked in bewilderment, "Hey! How can you talk about a dying child like that?"

"Well, just look at him. He's not going to die, Lady Arman."

"And what do you mean, 'child'? He's the same age as you, that cunning little...! Anyway, yes, it looks like he will survive."

"Why do you all sound upset about that?"

"Honestly, during that short period we shared the same room..."

Did something happen?

No. 2 and No. 3 paused and gave each other long-suffering looks.

Something happened, then.

For some reason, I could see the elders' long-suffering expressions overlapping with theirs.

Glenn, what the hell did you do to them?

"He's different from the way he acts in front of you. His bratty attitude was as quick as ever, even when he was weak from being hypnotized."

"It was absolutely ridiculous in so many ways." No. 3 shook her head. She added that feeling any type of affection for him was more shocking to her.

"Well, His Majesty isn't interrogating us, so it's all good if he isn't dead."

The way they regarded someone who had almost died so apathetically, just because of those reasons, was a little strange. But, well, they were the spies, and it seemed like Glenn had been an asshole. I wasn't sure what the fairies were doing, but I guessed that Glenn would suffer greatly afterward.

But it's karma, Glenn. I laughed awkwardly.

Charlemagne observed me silently before saying, "Did something change?"

"Oh." Jolting back to my senses, I answered, smiling widely, "My heart doesn't race anymore!"

My heart was never going to send me warnings in such an unnatural way again.

"I found the seal of the lord of the house." I sniggered evilly. "I'm going to brag to that asshole, Baron, when I get back."

"T-to someone who is being tortured?" No. 1 asked, instead of Charlemagne, who became speechless.

I smiled even more widely and nodded.

"Your heart doesn't race?"

"Not anymore."

"That's sad to hear," Charlemagne said.

I leaned away from him so I could see his face properly. "Sad? Why?"

"Because my heart races when I see you, but you're saying yours doesn't."

"Huh?"

"Am I wrong?"

Are you... Are you crazy?

Charlemagne looked indifferent, with a faint smile on his lips, but I detected the tiniest hint of sulkiness in his voice.

"I'm not talking about that kind of thumping!"

"I know." He let out a "hm" as he avoided my eyes.

"Are you sure you know?"

"Yeah."

Then, what was that silence earlier? I supposed that he was half-joking, but it was funny because he was half-serious as well. My lips quivered as I controlled my smile, and I poked his arm.

"My heart was surprised earlier, and right now..." I kissed him lightly on his cheek. "My heart is cheering."

As I pulled back, he kissed my lips as if he had been waiting to do so, and then gave a relaxed smile. "I know that, too."

I couldn't find a trace of sulkiness in the teasing smile on his face. He was so cute, I thought I would die.

"Ahem, ahem."

"Haaa..."

"I want to go home."

"Your Majesty, I shall lay down my life and attack the dark wizards myself."

Hearing the chancellor say with such gravity that he would rather die than watch us flirt was hilarious. I laughed silently as I leaned back after our kiss.

Now, all that was left was for Glenn to open his eyes.

Just then, the light that had been glowing over him faded, and the fairies' eyes snapped open.

"I don't wanna give it to the earth! Let's give it to Lettie!"

"It's half a fairy!"

They poked at something on the ground. I sprang to my feet and hurried over. When I looked closer, I saw a tiny baby fairy the size of my palm.

Argh! I grabbed my heart at how illegally cute it was, and the fairy boys shouted.

"Lettie! Lettieee! We did good!"

"We made a little brother!"

"It's ours now! No, it's Lettie's!"

Dazed, I held the baby fairy they dropped into my hands. No. 1, 2, and 3 gathered around me.

"Oh…"

"How cute!"

"Wow, so this is a baby fairy?"

Forgetting that they despised Glenn, they all looked fondly at the newborn fairy.

"I've heard that the Rashahels were close to fairies, but

this..." the chancellor murmured, his eyes full of amazement as he gazed at Glenn,

A calm, sparkling silence filled the air.

Eventually, the fourth fairy opened his eyes.

CHAPTER
ONE HUNDRED AND THIRTY-ONE

"Glenn?"

I hesitated for a moment, wondering what I should call the newest fairy, but then decided to just call his name.

"Humm…" Glenn, who was yawning as he rubbed his eyes, blinked. "Hmph."

As the people around me watched the cute fairy stretch, their expressions shifted.

"The fairy won't have a horrible personality, will it?" No. 3 asked first, looking half-entranced.

"Hmm, I don't know." I forced down my laughter at his serious question and carefully held Glenn.

Bonk! Glenn fell over in my hands and looked around in surprise.

Eeee! He's so cute! Maybe it's because I started getting attached? My heart dropped to my feet when I thought he was going to die.

I never intended to leave him to die—even if I *had* thought to use him as bait. I mean, he was probably a distant relative on Scarlett's mom's side.

Thank god... he's alive.

"Sis... ter...?" Glenn, who was wide awake, called to me in his bright voice.

"Huh?" I grabbed my throbbing heart as his little face gazed at me, and then I paused. "I-it appears he hasn't lost his memories." He said "sister," so that much was certain.

The chancellor's and the spies' faces immediately turned cold.

"The little devil is still the same."

"How interesting!"

"This is interesting to you? That little devil is now a majestic fairy!"

I guess Glenn acted even more odiously than I had imagined.

"Hmm." Charlemagne looked at the baby fairy disapprovingly.

Instead of asking what he was refraining from saying, I covered Glenn with my palm. The fairy boys giggled and flew in between me and Glenn as they shouted.

"That's the youngest! The last one!"

"It's a baby."

"Lettie, did we do a good job?"

Their little grins were so cute that I kissed each of them on the forehead. "Yes. You're the best."

"Humph!" Glenn crossed his short little arms as his smooth forehead wrinkled. He glared at Gill, Nell, and Bell with a displeased look on his face.

"You did well too by staying alive, Glenn." I kissed Glenn on his baby forehead, pretending I didn't know anything.

The baby fairy Glenn froze. As I smiled, watching his cute little face turn bright red, another face came close to mine.

"Lett, what about me?" Charlemagne asked.

"What?"

"I found the door that leads to the dark wizards' central base."

"Charl?"

"And I protected you."

"I know. Thank you."

"And?"

When I cocked my head in confusion, a calm smile appeared on his face. I flinched when I saw that his expression was soft but had an odd coldness to it.

Why is he...?

"Oh." I looked at him with narrowed eyes. Then, I followed his face as he sullenly pulled away and kissed him on the lips.

"Kya!"

"Again!"

"You kissy kissers!"

"Dang it."

I thought I heard a word that shouldn't be in a fairy's vocabulary, but I ignored it. I gave him another peck, and the corners of Charlemagne's mouth curled upward as he lightly bit my lip.

"Your Majesty! You said you found the door to the dark wizards' headquarters? Oh my!" the chancellor shouted. "We have no time for this! It's! The place! You've been searching for! For so long!"

Nobody replied, but the chancellor continued.

"We! Need to go! Immediately! Wait, we must contact the capital first."

Thanks to the chancellor's loud voice taking me out of my thoughts, I gently moved away from Charlemagne to look at the chancellor. Charlemagne's face bore a satisfied smile and his eyes lingered on me for a moment before moving to the chancellor's face as well.

I felt the temperature around us drop a few degrees and hugged the fairies closer to my chest. "You should contact the capital, Chancellor."

"Right," he answered in a dejected voice.

Is he sulky because we're not taking him with us? But taking him makes me anxious. I think he's the most vulnerable to the dark wizards.

"You're coming with us to the other side of that door?"

When I looked at him sympathetically, Charlemagne put the fairies, who were rubbing their little faces on my chest, one by one on the ground.

The spies also expressed their concerns. "Will it be all right?"

"Lady Scarlett, why don't you stay here?"

"Oh, I'm not saying we should go through the door. I'm saying don't worry about me."

"Come again?"

I grinned and showed them the seal of the lord of the house.

It was as Isar had relayed. It wasn't tangible, as it referred to a power. A warm energy began flowing from my heart. Everyone's eyes widened when they saw my fingertips sparkling with the gold-white power.

"If I take this..." I walked over to where Glenn had been lying on the ground. There had been a puddle of black blood earlier and now the ground was charred. I lowered my fingertips to the ground.

"Lett."

"It's all right. Come and watch."

The fairies, who had been glaring and bawling at Charlemagne, whooped and shouted when they saw me restore the grass.

"The grass isn't dead!"

"It's fresh! Lettie! Give us fruit! They'll be more delicious right now!"

"Froot... I wanna froot, too. Sister... sister is ha... happy." There was a hint of excitement in Glenn's shy voice.

I confidently pointed to the grass that had returned to its state of before the incident. "What do you think?"

"Is it a sacred power? No, it's more like..."

"To think that it would show such a phenomenon even though it isn't a sacred power."

"A sacred power would only turn back the time of the object, so the grass wouldn't be this fresh. What in the world is it?"

The spies were intrigued, and the chancellor was deep in thought.

Charlemagne, who had been staring hard at the grass, spoke. "Seeing as how it looks cleaner than any other area, it looks like purification to me. Is that right?"

"It is. And it isn't just this power. There are a whole bunch of different abilities. Oh, and when I said we shouldn't go to the other side..." I glanced at the place Charlemagne had come from. "I mean that I have a feeling we shouldn't go there right now."

"Why not?" Charlemagne tilted his head.

"You said you're skilled at detecting dark wizards, right? I think I know what you mean now. This is how you must feel. I feel something gross from that direction over there, for no reason at all. It's as if I just saw a cockroach," I murmured.

Everyone blinked.

"A cockroach?" Charlemagne asked, bemused.

I nodded. "You know, when you see a cockroach, you get that feeling."

"What feeling?"

"Like it's gross and you hate it, but more than that, you want to get rid of it as soon as possible."

"Ah." Charlemagne nodded.

"Like the only thing you want is to kill it."

"Mm, yes, exactly."

Charlemagne and I both stared in the direction of the door. Like we were looking at a cockroach.

The chancellor and the spies, who were gazing blankly at us, began to whisper to each other.

"It's creepy how they're glaring over at the same place, side by side."

"They say married couples take after each other. Weren't they always like that, though?"

"It's like I'm looking at two demon lords."

"Opere is humming again. His Majesty must be in a very good mood right now."

Feeling the waves of the power of Arman wash over me, I opened my mouth. "Charl, do you remember?"

"Remember what?"

"That time the ancestors of the three houses helped us?"

The chancellor's eyes sparkled at my words. He was highly interested in what we had gone through inside the book. "I have been wanting to ask. What kind of help did they give you?"

"A little bit of this and that. Everything we needed to kill someone, I guess?"

"That's right."

I looked at the chancellor as I grinned, and he clamped his mouth shut. The three houses had given us a lot of help when we killed the tyrant in the book, but we hadn't seen the power of the lords of the houses or anything like that back then. I wasn't sure if it was because we were inside a book or because it was the past.

"They helped us without any reason, and I thought that was strange."

"It certainly was."

"But now, I'm thinking they helped us because they knew something."

I glanced at my holy object. It had hummed quietly when I used the power of the lord of Arman.

The holy object of the Goddess of Fire. It was an amazing holy object that had the powers of both healing and resurrection.

"I could feel the power resonating with my holy object."

Charlemagne looked at his ring—the holy object of the God of the Moon. Though we didn't know what its power was, we knew it was unusual because it belonged to the God of the Moon, who didn't exist in this world.

"Mine did that as well earlier."

"I see." I fell silent, thinking for a moment, and then smiled as I met Charlemagne's eyes. "You know, if the holy objects are related to the powers of the three houses…"

"Mm-hmm."

"I thought we had fallen into the dark wizards' trap when we were trapped in the book, but that might not be the case."

Everything was coming together like pieces of a puzzle.

It doesn't seem like a coincidence.

Charlemagne was already using the power of Kalior, and I had awakened the power of the lord of Arman. I didn't know about Rashahel, but I had a feeling they prepared something as well. And now there were these holy objects that reacted to the powers of the three houses.

I feel like I'm being used.

It was as though we had been chosen as heroes to defeat the dark wizards.

Apparently thinking the same thing, Charlemagne smirked coldly. "We need to find Baba."

"Right?"

He often made that kind of face when he talked about Baba.

It was time for our mysterious friend to tell us everything.

CHAPTER ONE HUNDRED AND THIRTY-TWO

"But before that," I smiled meaningfully as I turned to Charlemagne. "You got close to the entrance, didn't you? What did you see there, Charl?"

I need to talk about this first.

"Nothing." He glared sharply in that direction. "There was nothing I could see."

"Then what about something you couldn't see?"

"Something lunged at me."

Was it Cheryl Diel?

"I didn't check what it was and came straight here."

"Hmm." I narrowed my eyes in the direction of the door as I contemplated. "Lady Diel isn't here right now, is she?" I asked to make sure because I couldn't feel her presence now.

No. 1 shrugged. "No, we verified that. She wasn't at the banquet hall, either. We can't detect her presence at all."

"The problem is that we could tell that she was up to something but couldn't sense that she was a dark wizard," the chancellor said apathetically.

No. 2 and 3 nodded in agreement.

"But based on the circumstances, it is highly likely that the lady is a dark wizard."

"He's right."

Charlemagne suddenly spoke up. "Come to think of it, I left an important hostage over there."

"A hostage?"

"I captured a dark wizard, but I left him by the door."

"Eh?" *You did that on purpose, didn't you?* He didn't sound flustered at all.

"So," Charlemagne continued, unfazed. "If we go now, the door should be open. It's a door that only appears when a dark wizard is close to it."

"Wouldn't the thing that popped out from behind the door have taken him?"

"I don't know. I left him far from the door, so I should go and check."

I knew it. He did it on purpose.

"And you're going to go alone?"

"I'll quickly check and bring back the hostage before we go meet up with Baba."

"Meh. That's boring."

"Hmm?"

I shook my finger and my head, and Charlemagne blinked.

"What are you planning to do?"

I grinned and let out a giggle. "I think I need to use the power of Arman at least once so I can get a feel for it. Let's all go together."

The rest of the party looked at each other and then followed in the direction I was walking, looking intrigued.

"Bathroom, bathroom!" I hummed while I searched for a bathroom. "Let's see... Ooh!"

I saw a toilet over yonder. I nudged the power that protected the lord of Arman, and it began to react from within my heart. The power was something close to supernatural, and I had felt something similar before when I was inside the book.

More precisely, it felt the same as when I'd used the power of the Goddess of Fire. I didn't really need to practice using the power of the lord, to be honest, but I needed to test my limit at least once. The power of the Goddess of Fire wore out my body if I used too much of it, but that couldn't be helped because it absorbed people's injuries to heal them.

Not that I'm complaining since it has the power of resurrection to make up for that.

But still, the fact that I couldn't use it continuously was a flaw. The seal of the lord of the house was different, though. This power...

Follow the water main.

Telekinesis. Self-healing. I could use this type of basic ability without any limitations.

Let's move the most contaminated place entirely.

Only a legitimate lord or young master could use the power without restraint. And Scarlett Arman was certainly legitimate.

I'm a temporary lord at the moment, but Scarlett was designated as the young mistress when she was young, too.

There was a rushing sound from far away.

"Should we go now?" I turned around, smiling excitedly, and everyone shot me suspicious looks.

"What did you do?" Charlemagne asked hesitantly.

I grinned. "It's kind of gross, but I'll tell you one thing. When I nod once later, everyone needs to stand behind me. Otherwise, you'll be miserable."

"Don't say something like that in such a bashful w—Argh!"

No. 3 crushed her heel into the chancellor's foot as she shouted, smiling awkwardly, "Sh-should we leave, then?"

I nodded and asked Charlemagne to take the lead. He glanced at the bathroom and back at me, and then grabbed my hand to drag me away with an odd expression.

Charlemagne couldn't use the same speed he had used

during battle, so it took longer than expected to arrive at the door. The doorframe was standing in the middle of some broken stairs, and the dark wizard was unconscious and far away from it.

"He's not dead, is he?"

"Of course not."

"Ooh! There really is something sticking out of it."

I saw a hand dangling and flailing as it grabbed at the air and trembled. It was red—the hand itself was skin-colored, but it seemed to be covered in blood.

"There used to be a door, but it looks like it was broken off," Charlemagne whispered in my ear.

I twitched because it tickled, and his lips curled into a leisurely smile.

We took some time looking at the doorframe, and when I nodded, everyone moved to stand behind me. The stuff that had followed me through the pipes had gathered enough under our feet.

"I guess dark wizards can't overcome physiological functions, either."

There was a lot piled up. As I muttered seriously and contemplated life, the chancellor staggered. He retched, and No. 2 patted him on the back, looking pale. The chancellor looked even worse.

Charlemagne, who had noticed what I was going to do, held back a smile. "That place is a magical space and probably has no connection to the water main. How are you going to do it?"

"Don't worry! I have my boys."

The fairies, who were huddled in my arms and quietly chit-chatting with each other, looked up at me.

Glenn wore a serious expression. "Leeb it to me," he mumbled. "I stwong now."

"Okay, I'll leave it to you." *Just make it so it won't stink.*

"Nell, you rattle the dark wizard! And Bell and Gill, protect us."

"Okay!"

"Are we playing? Yay!"

"Lettie! This one's going to be our little brother! He was born a moment ago, but he's good at magic!"

"I am." Glenn tried hard not to look proud and snapped his fingers at the gallons of sewage I had gathered.

Gill, Nell, and Bell also snapped their fingers. That moment, I released everything. Cracks appeared in the wall.

Swish, swish! Swish...

The hand that had been flailing around mid-air halted, and the disgusting sewage water burst through the wall and cascaded into the door.

Down to the very last drop.

Kyaaagh! The uncanny scream of a woman echoed from far away.

"Ugh, it doesn't feel like she's dying."

"Feel?"

"Her scream. It isn't that satisfying." I wiped my nose with the back of my hand and turned around, feeling awkward.

The first thing I saw was everyone with their mouths stupidly hanging open. *Eh? Why are they making that kind of face over a little prank? They're the tyrant's advisors.*

I spoke sulkily to their blanched faces. "All I did was return the foulest thing in the estate to where it belonged. Why, did I go too far?" *Was bathroom sewage too much?*

They shook their heads fiercely.

"Your aim was perfect." Charlemagne was the only one who clapped as he smiled calmly.

Well, that's all that matters!

I giggled and pointed to the unconscious dark wizard. He was now completely fine thanks to Nell's help, and No. 1 picked him up like a sack of potatoes.

I've done everything I needed to do.

I looked around the estate before exclaiming energetically, "Let's go to Baba now!"

We resumed our journey to the war zone.

Behind the door, Cheryl gritted her teeth when Charlemagne left. Her original plan had been to kill Glenn and use his death to curse the others.

I was going to present them with nightmares, starting with the curse.

While it wouldn't have lasted long with those fairies around, it was the best way to torment them.

How the hell did things turn out like this? And so soon, too!

She never dreamed that things would end this way when they'd just arrived and had one banquet dinner. And why had that wench collapsed? Cheryl hadn't done anything to her.

Did she faint because she saw the corpse? No. Scarlett Arman isn't that fainthearted. Then why? And why did that dark wizard try to assassinate her without permission the moment she collapsed?

He served the silent dark wizard, so he didn't listen to Cheryl.

The tyrant obviously wouldn't stay still after being provoked like that!

But Cheryl had used her wits at the last minute to make another move. This entrance was a secret passageway, but it was open to any other dark wizard. It wasn't one that only the leading three members used, so revealing it wouldn't be a loss if she could take some of their party with her.

If they just step inside, not even the tyrant will be able to use his full strength.

It would be the same even if the fairies came along. Not only that, but the silent one could also join her inside the base.

"I'll suck out all the water from your bodies." *As long as any one of you falls into my trap.*

However...

"Kyaaagh!"

Sploosh! Crash! Splatter!

She hadn't caught anything with her hand and was now covered in sewage.

"Ugh! That little wench!"

Their base turned into an uncleaned bathroom in the blink of an eye. Unfortunately, Cheryl's powerful magic evaporated all the water from the rush of sewage that had crashed through the door. Screams and howls echoed within the walls of the once quiet dark wizard headquarters.

Those screams went on for a long time.

CHAPTER
ONE HUNDRED AND THIRTY-THREE

A breeze settled on the leaves. Baba finished his inspection of the barrier around the Mirror and slowly got to his feet.

"Where to now?" he asked, his dazed pink eyes narrowing in assessment.

To the capital or to the war zone? His god had said that something was going to happen in both places. A moment later, Baba made up his mind.

"I suppose it's better if I join them first."

Eventually, he started walking in the direction of Scarlett's party, which was heading toward the war zone.

Count Ruman gave orders to the commander, his knights, and Isar Arman the minute he returned home.

"You have to protect it."

The palace and the Arman estate were empty. There were many people inside, but their masters weren't there. Now that he had seen the dark wizards' power for himself, he knew that the houses where the master was absent weren't safe.

"Can you do it?"

"I must." Isar nodded from the other end of the communication bead, where he was situated at the Arman estate. He said to Count Ruman, "I know this estate better than Scarlett, and the elders are here as well."

Adrian and Brian weren't the only elders at the estate. The other elders had solved most of the issues in their own territories and promised Isar that they would come to the estate when he contacted them.

The problems weren't serious enough to take up too much time anyway. The soldiers that Adrian had sent out to find goblin treasure had returned home safely. Then, they were formally hired by Cidian to officially work in his territory. They still needed to investigate why Cidian's lands were emitting poison and why the young men had died. But that problem would probably only be solved once they took down the dark wizards.

Dion's golems that had trespassed on Brian's lands had been remodeled to be used as guardians in every territory. A new embankment was to be made on River Two, and the emperor had given his permission to raise the underwater creatures. The elders could come up to the estate now that all their conundrums had been solved.

What a relief.

The elders of Arman were by no means experienced politicians, but they were well-versed in other areas. They were reliable in times of crises like these.

No, not reliable but...

Isar shuddered as he remembered the chilling looks that fell over the elders' faces when he had informed them that the temporary lord of the house was being targeted. They never forgot to add "temporary" when they talked about her, but it seemed that they had already accepted Scarlett as the lord. That was good, but...

Their gazes were so menacing, the old geezers.

They'd all wanted to come, but Isar barely managed to convince them that they couldn't all leave their territories, so it was decided that Adrian, Brian, Dion, and Elphine would come.

"Ugh." Isar thanked the gods once more that he wasn't the lord of the house.

I'd probably die early if I saw those eyes too often. Only someone like Scarlett could have them wrapped around her finger.

"Lord Isar?" Count Ruman called suspiciously to Isar, who had suddenly shuddered and sighed.

"Oh, it... it's nothing." Isar halted the train of thoughts

that had moved on from the scary grandpas to praising his sister and waved his hand.

"Let me know if you need any help."

"We really will be all right, since we also have protective spells around our estate." Still, the dubious feeling lingered. "And the elders will be here," Isar repeated.

"Ah, when you say elders, you mean…"

"The hidden powers of Arman, so please don't worry."

The legendary stories of their younger days were spread far and wide across the continent, so they weren't exactly "hidden," but oh well.

Isar tried hard to sound confident as he concluded, "We'll have no problem holding down the fort until Scarlett returns."

Emperor Charlemagne's advisors were Isar's immediate superiors. *They'll stomp all over me if I don't look competent.*

"All right, then." Count Ruman shut off his communicator, looking more reassured.

Isar sighed in relief. *That man.* He may have been a crybaby in front of the emperor, but he could also be a tyrant with a whip in front of other people. While the chancellor was someone who solved problems with his own hands, Count Ruman was incredibly skilled at making other people solve them.

Knock, knock.

"Young master."

"Yes, Vector." Isar opened the door and greeted the butler.

"Are they here?"

"Yes, young master. All four have been invited inside."

"Let's go."

Adrian and Brian had been stuck at the estate as they were about to leave, and now, the elder with elf-blood, Elphine, and the magical researcher, Dion, had arrived.

When the fainthearted Isar opened the door to the reception room, the four elders' piercing eyes glared at him. He smiled awkwardly as he greeted them.

"Thank you for your assistance." There was no proof that dark wizards were going to attack, but they'd gathered anyway since there could be a threat. "It is very reassuring."

To be honest, the only job they would have now was to take a look around the estate.

"Please rest, and you can call me when you inspect the place. I shall be in my office working."

Elphine composed himself and spoke solemnly. "Young master, we are actually here to make our reports personally." His words were ominous.

"Reports?"

The four elders exchanged looks. "You know how we decided to remodel the golems so they could be used as guardians?" Dion continued. "The modifications would have been completed more quickly, but..."

"Yes?"

"There was a researcher who wasn't a part of my team."

"What do you mean?"

"Well, we were very careful when we researched our doll—I mean, the golems—to make sure they would be extremely obedient. But when we investigated why they had gotten out of control, he was the culprit."

Isar had assumed that the dark wizards had a hand in it, but he didn't imagine that they would have planted someone right at the heart of the elders' territory.

"How did you not know?" The words had come out more accusingly than he had meant for them to, but Dion continued as though it didn't matter.

"He killed one of our researchers and wore his skin. Did you know that dark wizards can't spend much time inside the Arman duchy? He periodically drank holy water so he could stay there."

"Holy water?" Isar's mouth fell open.

"It means the Temple and the dark wizards have colluded together," Adrian explained in a cold voice.

"That's not all," Elphine said. "They most likely caused the flooding of the river as well."

"How? What would cause a river to flood without using black magic?" The elders would have noticed if they had, so it made sense that they didn't use any.

Elphine cocked his head. "It seemed as though they weren't only using black magic, but the flooding wasn't a natural phenomenon either, so I went to ask the elves. I came here after I heard what they had to say."

"And?"

"They say that a god was involved."

Isar closed his mouth. He didn't know what to say.

"Wh-why would a god do that?"

"They also ruled out any clerical powers, so that only means one thing."

"Which is?"

"You might not have heard anything about the one they call the devil, young master. That one has been sealed, so only the ancient elf elders remember that god."

"What if..." Brian started, looking serious, "the dark wizards, the Temple, and the sealed devil." His eyes shook fleetingly. "What if they are all working together?"

A heavy silence followed his words.

"You said there is no solid proof that the dark wizards will attack this place, but I think otherwise."

Isar didn't respond.

"If I were them, I would have the Temple make a move first. Even though they are less powerful, they still have some tricks up their sleeves."

Isar immediately understood. He knew what The Temple's last card was.

Heresy designation.

The Temple served any and every god. Because of that, no matter how corrupt or financially decrepit they were, they could mentally influence the people of the continent immensely. At least, that was the case for now.

If they publicly attack the Imperial Palace and the House of Arman as heretics...

Things would change if they were dealing with the Temple instead of the dark wizards.

"That is why all four of you are here."

Brian and Adrian were here to strengthen their defenses. Elphine was detached from humans through his elf heritage, so he would be useful. Dion was here because magical researchers were on the same level as wizards, so the Temple couldn't treat them rashly.

"There's no evidence that they will resort to such

measures. But we should assume the worst when we make our move."

Brian nodded slowly.

Isar groaned.

"Young master?"

He turned right back around to find the communication bead. He needed to tell Scarlett what he had just learned.

ONE HUNDRED AND THIRTY-FOUR

"What's wrong, Lett?"

I turned around at Charlemagne's question.

"Something feels strange." I thought someone had called my name, but it was probably my imagination. *I wonder if it's because we're in the dark wizards' lair. Something feels off.* I shook my head. "Do you think the people who went home have arrived safely?"

"Why are you asking that?" Charlemagne asked calmly.

"I mean, it's clear that a dark wizard drove us into these lands." We'd never seen Cheryl directly use dark magic, but it was certain because of all we had been through. "She also probably faked being attacked by demons and monsters. And if that kind of performance is possible, then we need to assume that she can control them. Nell did say that nothing happened on their way back, but..."

"That was unexpected, yes."

It was as he had said. She could have attacked the people going home before they reached the capital, but she didn't do that.

"Or perhaps her goal wasn't to simply kill them."

I furrowed my brows at his words because I suddenly thought of something.

"The Temple is in the capital."

"Yes." Charlemagne, who had no reason to feel pleased about anything, gave a meaningful smile.

"Charl?"

"It's going to be all right. They exist for that reason."

Is he talking about his advisors who returned? Or about the knights as well?

But then again, the capital was his home base, so there probably was no need for concern.

"I did get in contact with Isar before we came here. He seemed worried about us, so I don't think there was anything going on at his end."

"That's good to hear." Although things could have changed within a day. *I'll get in touch with him anyway, just in case.* I also had to tell him that I found the seal of the lord of the house.

Thinking about several things at once, I said brightly, "Did you collect all the evidence?"

"Yes, though it won't change much."

"But if you have evidence, people won't say anything about it like they did before." I was talking about the time when the dark wizards massacred the Masiar family and blamed it on him.

"Lett," Charlemagne said, slightly awkwardly. "Making my reasons for killing someone public—"

"Won't change anything? Charl, listen to me."

Most people couldn't deal with dark wizards because there weren't many who had the ability to. Only a selected few could take action to thwart their evil deeds. But reputation was a different matter.

"Tell me the truth, Charl. How many people unrelated to dark wizards have you killed?"

I pretended to push my non-existent glasses up my nose as I pressed him. *I can't approve of everything he has done just because we're in a relationship.*

Charlemagne watched me for a moment before replying nonchalantly, "My family."

"Not them." *They were the ones who tried to kill you!*

"Then, nobles who committed transgressions?"

"It's up to you to decide the punishment for breaking the law, so let's not discuss that right now."

I mean, it *was* excessive. Even with the elders of Arman. Their transgressions didn't have to go as far as they did, but they were all executed in the novel.

They shouldn't have hidden their actions from him, but they did it because of his reign of terror.

Imposing the emperor's authority was necessary in this world, and I knew that making examples of people to instill fear was a way to do that, but...

You can't rule the people with fear alone.

Once I organized my thoughts in my head, I nodded and lifted my chin. "Who else?"

"What I want to know is what you're thinking."

"Tsk, tsk! Hurry up and tell me. I think they're almost done packing."

That's the face he makes when he's trying to hold back his laughter. I gave him a frightening glare, and he quickly smoothed out his expression as he realized the scariness of a girlfriend.

"The rest were dark wizards."

"See? Charl, if you remove the dark wizards, who *had* to die, from the list of people you killed, then your notoriety will lessen a lot."

"But—"

"I'm not telling you to make excuses after all this time. I'm telling you to uphold your cause from now on."

Dark wizards had to be killed. Though I hadn't seen it for myself, the evil they perpetrated in secret was the kind that had completely discarded all traces of humanity.

I didn't hurl a waterfall of crap at them for no reason.

It wasn't that I thought they deserved to die because they tried to kill me. I had heard the way they spoke and saw what they did in collusion with the duke. Those kinds of atrocities were a frequent occurrence with the dark wizards. They didn't hesitate to sacrifice people. The very act of becoming a dark wizard required a living sacrifice in the first place, so every dark wizard was, at the very least, a murderer.

"Listen to me, Charl."

"Okay." He smiled tenderly and meekly leaned forward.

I gazed straight into his eyes and spoke calmly. "While only a minority can kill them, the majority absolutely has to want to kill them."

"I understand."

"It has to be that way, starting now, if you want to stay on the throne."

"I don't really—"

"It isn't a position you can step down from just because you don't want to do it anymore." *People already think of you as a tyrant.* "I don't know about anything else, but I'm saying you can't be their common enemy. It worries me!"

Charlemagne paused. "You're worried?"

"What? Of course, I am! And I don't like it when people talk badly about you. I mean, I'll personally punish any badmouthing I hear, but this is something you need to be careful about and think about, Charl. Okay?"

He gazed at me silently. I shrank a little at his faded smile.

Was I too harsh?

But a moment later, he hugged me.

"Huh?"

"I..."

Love you? That's what's coming next, right? Because this mood...

My surprise only lasted a few seconds, and my eyes sparkled at my thoughts. I hugged him back even tighter and lifted my heels to ready myself for a kiss.

I'm ready! I stifled the wolfish giggle that threatened to escape my lips and delightedly waited for his next words.

Charlemagne burst out laughing and buried his face in my shoulder. It was so tickly that my toes squirmed.

"What?" I shouted.

"It's just that I can't breathe because you're hugging me so tightly."

I pinched his waist, totally disappointed, but due to his layers of clothes, only my feelings got hurt. He erupted into laughter again, and after a while, he slowly stepped away from me.

His blinding beauty shining with the remains of his laughter, he leaned forward and whispered in my ear, "I love you."

We packed everything we needed. Everything useful that we could find in the Diel lands, that is.

If we had at least one object imbued with dark magic, that would be best, because it would be evidence.

"We turned the entire place inside out!" No. 3 shouted excitedly.

"Especially money! And food! And expensive clothes!"

"Perfect!" I clapped loudly, looking at her proudly.

"Let's get going, then!"

To the war zone where Baba is.

At that moment, Isar made contact via the communication bead. "Scarlett!"

"Isar?"

Fairy Glenn fluttered over with the communication bead, pretending it wasn't heavy for him. I looked carefully at Isar's face.

"Is there something wrong?" I suddenly felt anxious.

"The elders are here."

"Why?"

"Just in case. Don't make that face. Nothing's happened yet."

"Oh, good." Relieved, I continued, "Who's there?"

"Adrian, Brian, Elphine, and Dion."

"Tell them I'm grateful."

"They say there's no need. They think the Temple will make its move, and there's the possibility of a heresy designation."

Charlemagne's eyes flashed coldly as he watched the communication bead.

"I suppose they're planning to mention the Imperial Palace, too."

"I wanted to let you know. Just come home safe once you finish your business."

"Okay," I answered before ending the connection on the communication bead. Then, I made up my mind.

When I meet up with Baba, I'm going to kidnap him first.

CHAPTER
ONE HUNDRED AND THIRTY-FIVE

Count Ruman had told Scarlett some time ago that only two of the oldest families on the continent are left now.

Among them, it was said that the founder of Kalior was the dead God of the Winter Winds.

"A dead god?"

"It means they've become human."

He was said to have the power to transcend dimensions.

"Oh, don't tell me that the Armans and the Rashahels were gods, too!"

Those three were said to be the oldest families on the continent.

The story was interesting because up until then, I hadn't known why the House of Arman was so powerful.

"The Arman progenitor was the dead God of Prophets and Travelers, and the Rashahel progenitor was the dead Goddess of the Clovers."

The Temple had the inherent authority to proclaim to the entire continent that a certain party or group of people were heretics. If someone was labeled a heretic, they would receive all the unpleasant attention of everyone around them.

And that's putting it lightly.

Luckily the previous Scarlett still had common sense about that. She was a noble, after all, and this was one of the things that nobles had to be most careful about.

To be honest, I didn't understand this incredibly religious concept. It was hard to think of it along the lines of that terrifying war in the Middle Ages. The Temple didn't have as much power during those times, but this was far graver than I had imagined.

According to the video that played before my eyes, anyway.

"Heresy designation, Your Majesty?"

"It shouldn't be a problem."

"What do you mean, 'It shouldn't be a problem?' Have you lost your mind?"

In the video, Charlemagne was speaking coldly to Count Ruman, who was crying.

"You seem to be the one who has lost his mind, Count."

Though his voice was calm, there was an ominous energy flowing around Charlemagne. I continued to watch the video with my lips slightly parted, and I became kind of curious.

I understand that these videos play because of the Arman power of prophecy, but why do they show me the past as well?

Like the time one video showed me Glenn Masiar's past. And the futures the videos showed me were possible futures from the novel. But the video that I was seeing now was different.

"Designating the heir of a dead god as a heretic would be a gamble for the Temple."

"I wonder. If they were smart enough to worry about that, they wouldn't be threatening me like this right now."

I had never read this conversation between Count Ruman and Charlemagne in the original novel. I was sure of it—because I had never heard "heresy designation" being mentioned in it.

"Hmm." I decided to just classify it as a hidden side story in the novel.

Upon hearing their conversation, I abruptly remembered the time when, on the way back from dealing with the two elders' problems, Count Ruman had told me a story about the heirs of the dead gods.

I was familiar with it now. The most important thing was that the legend of the founders was widely known across the continent. That was probably why the Temple couldn't openly show enmity toward the three houses.

That was their only choice because they served many gods. The main god held the highest position, but they also served many others—even though there were few who had sacred powers because the gods were asleep.

It was also said that any clerics who had sacred powers had been kicked out long ago. I always thought Baba was one of them.

But that probably isn't all there is to him...

Charlemagne's voice from the video cut through my thoughts.

"Perhaps I should make public what the Temple has done."

"Come again?"

Unlike Count Ruman, who was looking confused, I understood the moment I heard his words. *Yes! Exactly!*

The video ended with Charlemagne slowly wiping down his blade as he spoke about everything the Temple had done to him and Cheryl. He was most likely telling the count to spread the information far and wide.

I smiled brightly.

"Are you awake?" asked Charlemagne, sitting next to me as I lay there. We had made camp for the night on our way to see Baba.

"I should get some sleep, but I can't fall asleep," I

murmured. I was buried inside my sleeping bag in the warmest part of the campsite, with only my face poking out.

Charlemagne smiled down at me. His deep gaze gave me shivers. I poked out one of my hands as well, and he grabbed it as if he had been waiting for it. Interlacing our fingers, we looked up at the night sky.

"It would be brighter if there was a moon."

"It's bright enough since we have a campfire."

"It'd be even brighter."

"Is that so?"

It was fascinating to see the stars sparkling without the moon. It was pretty. I was silent for a while before I conveyed to Charlemagne what I had thought of after I saw the video.

We needed to drag the Temple's name through the mud before they labeled us as heretics.

"Since they're trying to go against the heirs of the dead gods, perhaps..."

"They may not be able to pronounce us heretics because they would worry about their reputation falling even further."

"Exactly."

"Brilliant."

"Don't you think? I might be a genius."

It was Charlemagne's idea, to be honest, but I took the credit for myself. Even though I just realized we had gone through none of the attacks that Charlemagne and Cheryl had in the novel.

"There's no reason for us not to play dirty if they're going to argue about something that doesn't exist, right?" I winked, and an odd expression crossed Charlemagne's face.

"Well, the first rumor that I want to spread is..." I told him an exaggerated version of the things that the Temple had planned to do to Charlemagne and Cheryl in the novel.

He listened to me silently and then gave me one of his rare speechless looks. "It's so detailed."

"Oh, I know."

There was a bark of laughter from the chancellor, who was lying a short distance away. When I looked over, wide-eyed, I saw him curled up and sniggering to himself. Then, as he felt our eyes on him, he fell silent as if nothing had happened.

Jeez.

"It would also be a good idea to restore the reputation of the true clerics while we're at it."

I clapped in agreement. Baba was probably already in the war zone. *And I'm going to kidnap him and take him home...*

Now that all the old true clerics had disappeared, Baba was the only one left. If we were going to blatantly take him back with us, Charlemagne's idea was a good one.

The next day, we arrived at the lake that was said to reflect the moon, where Baba would have arrived first. But...

"There's nothing there."

"It looks like a normal lake to me."

"Your Majesty? Lady Scarlett? What is the matter?"

I turned to look at Charlemagne without saying anything. He nodded his head.

"Can the two of you see something?" Chancellor Clover asked cautiously.

We couldn't find the words to answer and just stared at the lake.

Varsha Brockel. Seriously, what the hell is he?

I could feel it. This place was full of Baba's energy. No, more precisely, I could feel the energy of Baba's sacred power, of his god. It was engulfing the entire lake. *Like he's trying to hide something.*

I could tell because I had felt this sensation inside the book. This wasn't something a human could do. The power was so strong that I would believe if someone told me it was done by a god.

Vmmm...

My bracelet and Charlemagne's ring vibrated faintly as

they glowed and then started to swell like they were going to explode.

"Huh? Oh, oh…"

However, we couldn't remove them no matter how hard we tried.

Hmm? This is unnerving.

"Charl, should we cut off my wrist and your finger and then stick them back on after?" *Well, I could* probably *do it.*

"You need the power of your holy object to do it."

"Oh yeah… And it'll look kind of gross if we don't have those body parts."

But at this rate, it felt like we would lose an entire arm, not just a wrist and a finger.

"Why are you two saying such terrifying things?" the chancellor muttered bitterly, and the spies took a step back away from us.

Putting those four, who were whispering about "birds of a feather" or whatever, on the back burner, we grimly glared at our holy objects.

What do we do?

Charlemagne furrowed his brows fiercely. "Lett. Opere is making a racket."

"Oh, the sword. It speaks to you now, doesn't it? What is it saying?"

Opere was the pitch-black sword with demon-like power that was actually a holy sword, right? It had been handed down from generation to generation of Kaliors and had finally met its rightful owner.

Charlemagne said it was annoying because it talked too much, though.

Still, it's been alive for as long as the House of Kalior, so wouldn't it know something about the situation we are in?

I gazed expectantly at Charlemagne.

"It keeps saying that the world will become perfect," he said, frowning.

"Perfect?"

"It says that's why we need to leave this place. That's what it keeps saying."

So, we can't let the world become perfect? The hell is it saying?

I stared at the sword for a moment. "Do you think that sword is ticklish?"

I have a feeling I should interrogate it.

CHAPTER
ONE HUNDRED AND THIRTY-SIX

– Aaaggghhh!

Charlemagne grinned as he listened to the comical screams coming from his sword.

"It can?"

He nodded when I asked him if the sword could feel sensations.

– Traitor!

"It's telling me I'm a traitor."

– Tattletale!

"Now it's calling me a tattletale."

"My, my. How rude." I smacked it, and the sword quivered.

– Stop! Stop it! You barbarian! Kya!

I couldn't hear what it was saying, but I could see it tremble whenever I touched it. *So, this sword is that child, right?*

Inside the cursed book, we had crossed paths with a young boy who was one of the forefathers of the House of Kalior, and his dream was to become a sword.

"What good is it to achieve your dream when you can't even remember the time you dreamed it?"

– What are you grumbling about? Master! Why aren't you taking my side? Make her stop this indecent behavior at once!

That's what the sword said, according to Charlemagne. *This sword is so funny!*

I smirked and tickled it for a long time. With nowhere to run, the ego sword finally waved the white flag to surrender.

"What is it saying?"

"Hmm." Charlemagne listened to Opere for a while. "In the perfect world, both the gods and people were perfect."

The spies and the chancellor gathered around us.

"But then, the world was split in half because that was the only way to seal one of the gods."

"A sealed god?"

"It must be talking about the god that the dark wizards want to release."

"That god wasn't always the devil. He was the main god."

"The *main* god?" asked No. 1 in a frightened voice.

And of course, he would be scared. The main god was the *God of Gods.*

"But the main god right now is the God of the Sun..."

"That god was the one who led the other gods to seal the devil."

No. 3 nodded sagely. "Out with the old, in with the new."

"They had to seal away the main god? Why in the world...?"

"Apparently, they had differing opinions."

"What kind of opinions?"

Charlemagne listened for a moment. "The devil wanted to take away free will from the people."

He proceeded to explain that the former main god made the extreme claim that humans did not need free will, and the other gods combined their strength to counter him. However, they couldn't rashly drag him down from his position, and the gods inevitably chose the path of sacrificing themselves.

"They made the devil believe it was a game and succeeded in sealing him, but most of the gods fell asleep, and the three great gods died as a result."

"And those three great gods were Kalior, Arman, and Rashahel?"

"Yes. They died because their mission was to protect the humans from becoming the victims of a gods' war."

"How does it know all of this when it doesn't even have its own memories?"

"I wondered that, too."

Charlemagne stared at Opere, and it trembled for a moment before it twitched.

"It says it heard from the savior who helped it turn into a sword."

Charlemagne's expression was odd, and I had a feeling I knew why.

"Don't tell me. Is Baba the 'savior'?"

"It says it doesn't know his name."

Maybe he isn't?

"All it knows is that the man was a pink-haired, pink-eyed high priest."

Wait, that's basically the same thing! I had only known one pink-haired, pink-eyed person in all my two lives.

"How old do you think he is?" I sighed.

"I don't know," Charlemagne responded unconcernedly, "but I do know that I'm going to give him hell when I see him."

"Why is that, Your Majesty?" the chancellor, who had been listening with interest, piped up.

Charlemagne's reply was indifferent. "There's no way that kind of man would have let the dark wizards steal something he was protecting."

"Agreed."

I nodded sullenly. "We must assume that he let them steal it. If that's true, it's highly likely that he already knew that we'd go inside the book, and about what the dark wizards were doing."

"How are we going to shake him down if he's such a powerful man?"

A momentary silence followed. It appeared that even Charlemagne was stumped.

I smiled as I said what I was thinking. "We have to force him to make a move." I didn't know what it was, but I had a feeling he was methodically doing something. "I think he wants to help us grow, not to kill us."

"So...?" asked No. 2, looking anxious.

"Well, that means he isn't against us, so at least we don't have to worry about dying."

"True."

"Basically, we'll be fine even if we do something like this!"

"Like wha—Ahh!"

With No. 2's scream playing as background music, I enthusiastically threw a rock at the lake.

The rock that whistled through the air was full of the power of my holy object, which had been humming and glowing for a while now. The moment the ordinary-looking rock arched through the air and hit the surface of the lake...

Boom!

"U-unbelievable," the chancellor groaned.

Only Charlemagne, who was examining the surface my

rock had hit with narrowed eyes, looked unconcerned. He turned to me. "Do you think it will break if I use a boulder?"

"I don't think it has to do with size."

"Ah." He looked down at his holy object offhandedly. It was the holy object of the God of the Moon, the ring that no one knew the purpose of—only that it glowed. Then, he let out a short laugh, which sounded a bit crazy.

"I get it now."

"Ooh!"

As I clapped, Charlemagne picked up a large boulder and chucked it like it was a ball of cotton.

Kaboom!

Drawing a beautiful arch in the air, the boulder crashed into the spiritual force field that Baba had made with his sacred power.

I crammed stones, twigs, and leaves with my power and vigorously threw them at the barrier as well.

I'm so psyched! "Ahahaha! It's like a snowball fight!"

"What's a snowball fight?"

"It's something you do when it snows. You ball up the snow and throw it at each other. Next time it snows, let's turn Baba into a snowman, and then you and I can have a snowball fight, Charl."

"That sounds fun."

The "snowball fight" went on for a while.

Then, the chancellor suddenly fell back with a squeal. He scuttled a few feet back to where the spies were huddled and muttering about us, and they also exclaimed in surprise.

When I turned around with a grin, I saw a pink-haired figure looking at us agitatedly.

"Hey Baba, it's been a while."

Charlemagne pretended not to have noticed and picked up another rock. He threw it at the barrier with all his strength before turning around slowly, greeting Baba silently with cold eyes.

Baba stared blankly at me and Charlemagne before asking, "What are you d-doing?"

"It looked suspicious."

"So, you threw rocks at it?"

"Uhm yes, because the lake was pretty?"

"Hey!"

"Ow, my ears. Why are you yelling?" I snapped at him sulkily, and Baba flung away his usual dazed attitude and started fuming.

Charlemagne picked up another rock and muttered to himself, "I mean, we wouldn't be doing this if *somebody* had told us what he was hiding."

"I know, right?" I agreed wholeheartedly and took out a

piece of candy from my pocket. "There would be no reason for me to let my sacred power flow into this piece of candy if *somebody* would just spill the beans."

Both the candy and Charlemagne's rock harbored even more power than any of the other things we had thrown.

There will probably be a huge explosion this time if they crash into Baba's power.

"H-hide? Me? Wait!"

Ignoring Baba's shout, we drew back our arms and forcefully...

"Oh god, hold on! Argh! It's danger—"

...stopped in the middle of throwing the items in our hands. Instead, we grabbed Baba, who hastily sprinted toward us, from each side and made him slump between us.

He gazed up at us with a dazed expression, as if his soul had escaped his body. When I flashed him a bright smile, his pretty pink eyes wavered. We sat down on either side of him, with one hand holding him in place and the other clutching the rock and the candy.

"So, is the god you serve the God of the Sun?"

"What! How did you—"

"Ah, so you do serve him? Charl, ask him something."

"Are there any other true priests? You'll have to do it by yourself if there aren't."

"Do what?" Baba glanced nervously at the items in our hands with shaky eyes, looking a little lost. "Why don't you put those things down first? It's dangerous here."

"Why? What's so dangerous about it? What will happen if we break it?"

"You'll be sucked in!"

"How?"

Baba looked taken aback by my question, but Charl spoke up.

"If we get sucked in, then that means the heart of the world isn't on this side, but the other side."

"Do you know what the Mirror is?"

Mirror? All we knew was what Opere had told us, but it appeared that our fish had taken the bait.

It must have something to do with sealing the devil. Does that mean the split in the world is based on the Mirror? It must be a huge one.

Making this brief assumption, Charlemagne and I nodded casually.

"Of course."

"We know everything, so tell us everything. This is the last chance I'm giving you as a friend."

I forced down my laughter when I saw Charlemagne feigning innocence, with a chilling look on his face. I scowled, trying to keep my laughter at bay, and Baba flinched. He remained silent for a while, but eventually agreed to tell us everything.

We spent the whole afternoon talking.

Our interrogation—I mean, our conversation—came to an end just as scandalous rumors about the Temple began spreading like wildfire in the capital.

And finally, we found out.

Our world had split between the world on the other side of the Mirror and the world we were in.

Not only that, but the world inside the book we had traveled through was the real world that was trapped on the other side of the Mirror.

"Is that world a dead world?"

"Oh, you didn't know that? Well, time doesn't work in that world. They're in a constant loop, confined to the time when the gods fell asleep. I don't know how you found out about this. There's no way you could know..."

I sighed at the dawdling flow of words that slipped glumly from Baba's mouth.

"Becoming perfect" meant that if the Mirror was shattered, this world would combine with the real world. The people of this world were called "shadows," so that probably meant when the Mirror was shattered, the shadows would find their owners.

I can't believe that all of us in this world aren't actual people, but shadows.

It felt like I had been punched in the gut.

CHAPTER
ONE HUNDRED AND THIRTY-SEVEN

Shadows.

In other words, we were mere reflections in a mirror.

"Basically, if we shatter that Mirror, Charl and I will get sucked in. And we'll be absorbed into our real bodies?"

"Yes. We need to deal with the devil before you fuse with your bodies."

"What do you mean?" I asked incredulously. *We can't fuse with our bodies in this situation!*

Baba sighed. "The imperfect world is meant to disappear in due time. And that's not all."

According to him, the gods were planning to make this world the real one.

Once we've completely rid it of the devil, that is.

The devil was currently only contained, not destroyed. If he regained his powers, the world would be obliterated regardless of whether it became perfect or remained a fake.

"So, you're following a procedure, right?"

"Yes. If the devil dies here, the worlds can merge, with

this lake as the central point, because that point will move to the location where the main god died. Right now, there are more sleeping gods in the other world, so this world will merge into that one."

"The number of gods determines which world is real or fake?"

"Yes..." Baba responded sulkily, realizing that he had been baited into telling us everything.

"But how do we kill the devil if he's such a formidable being?"

"The devil won't be able to return to being a god as soon as the seal breaks. If the devil wishes to reclaim his divine status, he must first assume a human form. He'll descend into a human body first, and if he dies by the power of a god, he'll be gone."

"And if we fail?"

"We'll be trapped in this fake world. That's the worst-case scenario, though. Time doesn't flow in the real world anyway, so that world is as good as dead. We need to save this side instead."

"But even if the devil descends as a human, there aren't any gods who are awake right now. How can we kill the devil?"

"We have you guys."

"Us?"

"Oh! Do you mean to say," the chancellor chimed in as he approached us from a few feet away, "that the descendants of the dead gods are the answer?" His eyes were as sharp as a knife.

Baba nodded defeatedly. "The dead gods decided to stay on the other side of the sleeping gods, where the world was fake. Their powers were what maintained this shadow of a world to this day."

"Then, we are in a dire situation," the chancellor said, concerned. "Because the Rashahels no longer exist."

"What are you talking about?" Baba tilted his head in confusion. I had a feeling I knew what he was going to say next. "The powers of the three gods are at their peak, more than they have ever been."

"Excuse me?"

"You have no idea how much effort I've put in to achieve that."

"What do you mean?"

Baba shifted his gaze away from the bewildered chancellor. He looked at me and Charlemagne in turn before bobbing his chin in our direction. The chancellor's eyes grew wide.

I watched Baba intently with narrowed eyes.

I guess Scarlett Arman has a lot more Rashahel blood in her than I thought. However... I'm not the real Scarlett. I wonder if it doesn't matter if the body has a different soul.

As though he had read my mind, Baba winked at me.

So, there's something more, huh? But I couldn't ask him about it in front of the others. *It's fine, I'll ask him later.* The important thing was that there was a physical body from the bloodline.

I decided to move on to a different subject. "That means that Charl and I need to kill the devil in human form, and he'll probably possess the body of a dark wizard. It was something that we were planning on doing anyway."

"Hmm." Charlemagne grunted as though displeased about something. Then again, he was probably shocked by the fact that this world was fake. It felt like we'd been betrayed, but my shock was less than his since I was not from this world to begin with.

"Huh? Hang on." Suddenly, I felt that something was off. *Is this world really the fake one?*

Charlemagne opened his mouth to question Baba, apparently having thought the same thing. "How do you know?"

"Hmm?" Baba turned to look at Charlemagne, appearing far more peaceful than before.

"How are you so sure that this world is the fake one?"

"Because the world where time stopped flowing is the real one. The devil is the God of Time, so the world that was affected when he was sealed should be real."

"Why won't that world's time flow when the God of Time isn't even dead?"

Baba blinked. He was dazed and speechless for a moment, but then told us that his god didn't have an answer for that either. He continued, "Well, the slumbering gods are on the other side—"

"But the seal itself is on this side," I cut in. "Was the devil sealed in the fake world on purpose?"

"No, that isn't likely."

"Then, is it a coincidence?"

"I suppose."

"Isn't that a bit suspicious?"

"Why?"

"If I were the devil, I wouldn't have been defeated so easily. In addition, the houses of the dead gods who said they would go to the fake world were also on the other side."

Baba opened and closed his mouth a few times.

I spoke up in response to his flustered expression. "You saw them, too."

"Yes, I did, but I thought it was because of you two."

"But that's just your assumption, isn't it?"

"True." Baba frowned as he glared at the Mirror and sank into his own thoughts.

I exchanged looks with Charlemagne and mentioned another issue. "The holy objects that we found on the other side also exhibited their true powers only after we brought them into this world."

"Well, that's because they're real holy objects."

"Exactly. It felt like those very real objects genuinely came to life on this side." Even though my power of the Goddess of Fire was similar in both worlds. "The holy object of the God of the Moon, especially." It hadn't reacted in any way while we were inside the book.

I pointed at Charlemagne's ring with my chin. Baba's eyes traveled down to where it was glowing.

"I suppose this is unexpected for you," Charlemagne said as he watched Baba's eyes widen.

"The God of the Moon has awakened?" His murmur was tinged with bewilderment. "So suddenly?"

"If the ring's glow means that the god is awake, then I think he's been waking up every time I fight."

"Huh?" Considering how shocked Baba was, it seemed as though his god was still speechless.

"It appears the gods can't communicate with each other because they are asleep."

"That's true, but the moon doesn't exist in this world. There's no way that the God of the Moon can be roused."

"Why isn't there a moon here in the first place?" I asked, my brows furrowed.

"The God of the Moon was the first one to fall asleep," Baba replied vacantly.

"Why was it only the moon that disappeared when everything else didn't?"

"Because the moon helped the three gods die."

"Hmm." *So?*

Baba continued hesitantly, "The first to fall asleep was the moon, followed by your Goddess of Fire. So, the moon couldn't create a shadow."

"Nah, I think it's the opposite."

"The opposite?" Baba's eyes snapped wide open again.

"You said that the gods fell asleep to activate the Mirror." That meant the moon had already created a shadow. "The moon disappeared because its god fell asleep."

Baba, who seemed stupefied by the information, took a moment to curse out his god. He was sure his god was pretending to be asleep though he knew everything.

He sighed. "Then, if what you're saying is true, the real fact..."

"...is that the devil might actually be sealed in the real world, not the fake one," I continued.

"Ugh." I laughed awkwardly at his agonized groan.

Baba started muttering again, as if he were asking his god, "Wouldn't it be dangerous if the devil descends? If this is the real world, we need to destroy him before the seal breaks. Don't we?"

It seemed like he was going to keep pressing until he heard an answer. And a short while later, Baba revealed something surprising.

"We've been tricked."

"Hmm?"

Baba muttered again. I had never seen him like he was right now.

"Baba? What's wrong?"

"We were tricked."

"What?"

Baba spoke slowly, his face ghostly pale. "That's what my god said."

The gods had devised the most effective method for sealing the main god, whom they could never defeat.

The method was a game that would be played with the entire world.

Or rather, a hidden trap that made the devil think it was that kind of game.

The gods succeeded but ended up failing at the same time. The devil had fallen into their trap, but completely sealing him took longer than it did for most of the gods to fall asleep.

Thus, the devil had taken that opportunity to send all their holy objects into the fake world. He couldn't do anything about the object of the God of the Sun because that god wasn't asleep yet.

The devil even had the time to take a few measures to make everything look natural.

Good. Now we're on even footing.

The devil had laughed in secret. He felt that this dull world was starting to become slightly more amusing. Perhaps he might even be able to laugh as he watched those pathetic humans.

And now, after a long period of time...

At the same moment, the God of the Sun realized that he had been deceived, and the silent dark wizard smiled covertly.

CHAPTER
ONE HUNDRED AND THIRTY-EIGHT

However, that smile did not last.

"They had fairies with them?" The silent wizard scowled at Cheryl's report.

"They were quite powerful." The corners of her lips twisted. "But it wasn't enough to be concerned about."

"Are you sure about that?"

"Who do you think I am? You know what, forget that. Why didn't you tell me before?" The fairies weren't the ones who were grating on her nerves right now. She ground her teeth at what she had just heard from the other wizard.

"Scarlett Arman has Rashahel blood in her veins?!" she shouted.

"I only just found out as well."

"Don't lie to me!" Cheryl spat furiously, biting her lip.

The silent dark wizard and the weakest dark wizard did not have names, nor did they have any title to call each other by.

It was all for their god's descent. All so they could offer themselves wholly to his will.

Except that the one chosen to be the vassal is that one. The weakest dark wizard had been shelved due to his insanity.

But whatever the case…

"This is disconcerting. The dead gods haven't become weaker at all. We haven't been able to destroy any of them!"

There are only two of us left on our side!

"Our master will be wrathful."

The devil was the master who had given Cheryl new and powerful abilities when she was dying.

Would the two of them be able to defeat the heirs of the dead gods and the fairies? There were too many unsettling factors.

But even though she was displeased with the silent one, who had kept an important truth hidden from her, she had more pressing matters to focus on than her feelings.

"We have to hasten our master's descent as much as possible."

"You are right," the silent dark wizard replied in a low voice.

Goosebumps covered Cheryl's skin, and she instinctively felt a sense of danger.

"Where is the other one? We could probably keep the fairies occupied if we used his strength, even if he is crazy."

A grin twisted the silent one's face as he watched Cheryl

take a step back and search for the crazed dark wizard.

"There is no need. The descent has already begun, albeit inadequately." *My god will be making his move.*

"Master says he will gradually fill in the inadequacies as he demolishes everything. Thus..."

Faithful Cheryl Diel.

"You must now fulfill your duty."

That was the last voice Cheryl heard while she was alive.

The slumbering gods had expedited their attempts to destroy the devil, thinking that the world without the moon wasn't real. If the devil descended into a human body and an equal human killed his human form...

"We should have been able to obliterate him for good." The God of the Sun, who had begun talking after an extensive period of silence, spoke through Baba dejectedly. "That was why we had chosen you." They had also taken several other measures to help them kill the devil.

Scarlett and Charlemagne furrowed their brows, and Baba shrank a little. That was what they had done, but...

"We've been tricked. Every single one of us."

They'd thought this world was fake, but the other side of the Mirror was the replica.

"No wonder the gods slumbered for longer than we expected."

The God of the Sun had been worried that the other gods were asleep for too long, but they began waking when the holy objects came into this world.

"If this is the case, then the descended devil will be even more powerful."

These two will never be able to oppose him on their own.

"But we can't spend the entire time trying to prevent the seal from breaking!"

Though the seal had temporarily strengthened, it was bound to break one day. Consequently, the best way to crush the devil had become forever impossible.

Scarlett, Charlemagne, the fairies, and the four aides listened quietly to the God of the Sun as they racked their brains on what to do next.

Basically, the gods are just fighting among themselves.

It wasn't an entertaining story in the slightest, but to think that the Temple and the dark wizards were all part of that fight...

Charlemagne's expression was even darker because his entire life, he had been horribly scarred by those people.

Baba gritted his teeth as he watched the others' faces turn colder and colder. He had lived the life of a wanderer for so long, tied to his god. *But the god was being deceived the whole time? Damn it all.*

– *What do I do? What do I do?!* The holy voice of his god now only sounded obnoxious to him.

Scarlett, who had been quietly contemplating, tapped Baba on the shoulder.

"Hmm?" Baba turned his wan face toward her in the middle of listening to his god's laments.

"Baba. Why were we sucked into the other side of the Mirror?"

She was talking about the book. Why had they been sucked in if this world was the real one?

"Well, it's because I was there first."

"So, you're saying that it was the dark wizards who sent us into the book, but you planned for it to happen, right?" she asked gently, smiling.

Baba avoided Scarlett's eyes. "Th-that's right, but now that I think about it, the bodies that you and Charlemagne possessed changed their names to suit you both. I always thought that was strange, but maybe it was because you two were the real bodies after all."

"If we weren't the original bodies, then we could have been sucked into our 'real' bodies on the other side?"

"Yeah, but we made failsafe arrangements just in c—"

"That means the danger was still there, doesn't it? Come here, I'm going to beat you up."

Scarlett decided to do the honors because Baba would probably die if Charlemagne beat him, but of course, Charlemagne still landed a fair share of his own punches, too.

After a while, the God of the Sun spoke to Baba, who had been thoroughly beaten up, in a trembling voice. "Perhaps the moon is reflecting in the lake because the child of Kalior brought the holy object into this world and awakened the God of the Moon."

The God of the Sun felt a strange sense of déjà vu. He cleared his throat as he remembered the time he had been beat up by the God of the Moon and the Goddess of Fire. Then, trying hard to change the subject, he directed his speech towards the two humans, who now looked a little calmer now.

"W-we have to come up with a plan. In this state, we will lose the opportunity to rid this world of the devil forever. The situation is far graver now since there are no gods who can deter him."

"I wish I could send everyone and everything to the other side of the Mirror so those gods can fight it out themselves," Scarlett whispered to Charlemagne, who now looked infuriated. "Or I wish we could bring back all of the holy objects into this world."

Charlemagne paused just as he was about to agree. At his odd expression, Scarlett's eyes widened, apparently realizing what she had said.

"That's a good idea."

"Isn't it, Charl?"

There was no reason to hesitate if their world was the real one.

If we retrieved all the holy objects and found owners for them, wouldn't we be able to defeat the descended devil? Of course, we wouldn't just give the objects to anyone.

"That is a great idea! That would work! We even have fairies here, and they are our vestiges. If we gather our powers, all of that will be possible. What a brilliant child!" The God of the Sun glowed lustrously as he clapped. Baba wondered where his usual prim demeanor had gone. "Tell them to go find the book at once!"

"That makes all my efforts completely useless," Baba said, gritting his teeth. He was the one who had pulled all the strings on behalf of his god's orders.

At Scarlett's look, Baba began berating his god. "I can get the book back on my own, but you do know that even I can't bring back all the holy objects, don't you? And we can't send these two back inside again! Do you understand? Ugh!"

Under normal circumstances, the God of the Sun would have scoffed at Baba's tantrum, but he couldn't afford to do that right now. So, the god fervently coaxed and cajoled him.

"Please, child, I beg you. Who else do I have to rely on except you? What can I do to convince you?"

"I don't know, it might be too difficult for me. But if you help us, I could try."

"I shall help you with anything you want!"

Baba gave a mysterious smile at those words.

All good?

Yep. At Baba's look, Scarlett nodded prissily.

Charlemagne was still furious, but his bloodthirsty aura had lessened.

Baba flashed them a quick thumbs-up, and the three of them looked highly satisfied. Baba was now able to help his young, brilliant friends as much as he wanted.

"Well, then, I'll bring the book and the one who possesses it over to you, so wait for me at the capital."

"Okay! Come to the temple," Scarlett said.

"The temple?" he asked Scarlett.

Charlemagne answered in her place. "It appears that the god the Temple worships is the devil, so I figured we could publicly destroy it now."

The spies and the chancellor hugged and cheered in a corner.

"You have no idea how frustrated I was when all he did was block their source of income!"

"I never thought I would see the day that high priest would cry tears of blood!"

"Me neither!" *Sob!*

Baba smiled dazedly at their silly reactions, and then he was gone in a flash.

Time flew by rapidly, and a week later, Scarlett and her party were huddling in front of a small opening in the wall around the temple.

"What am I to do?" the God of the Sun murmured to himself as he watched the people gathered around. His eyes were fixed on Scarlett and Charlemagne.

Scarlett slipped through the opening first. Charlemagne practically glided through it. Calamity befell the temple.

As the god observed the scene unfolding before him, he continued his quiet mutterings. "One of them must be sacrificed."

No one heard his voice.

CHAPTER
ONE HUNDRED AND THIRTY-NINE

"A sacrifice is required to kill a god."

Just like how the three gods had to die to seal the devil.

"They're descendants, not actual gods, so a sacrifice is inevitable." The shabby and ragged god popped into his physical form in an empty space. He stared vacantly and let out a sigh. "Should I tell them? Or not?"

He had been planning not to. Even Baba didn't know this truth. He had wanted the survivors to live on, believing that the death of one of them was an unfortunate accident.

"If this place is the real world, then the one who must be sacrificed..."

The Kalior has the power of judgment and of the Winter Gale.

The Arman has the power of Rashahel's luck through her blood, in addition to the power of prophecy.

"...must be the Arman."

If this world was indeed the true world, Kalior had to remain. He had the power to exterminate evil. Compared to that, luck and prophecy didn't need a god to be in charge.

"In that case, it would be better to tell the child."

The child of Arman would understand.

"Hmm."

The truth was that this was something that the God of the Sun, who had taken the lead in sealing the devil because he dearly loved humans, didn't want to do at all. However, there was no one more suitable to kill the devil and challenge the dark wizards who worshipped him. Those two were also the only suitable candidates for a sacrifice, even if there were others with holy objects.

"I truly wish there was another way."

The God of the Sun's sighs became heavier.

Another week had passed. The city was in an uproar because of the many incidents that had happened in relation to the Temple.

First, the news about all sorts of atrocities that the Temple committed had spread like wildfire. The victims of the Temple's corrupt actions had posted anonymous notices around the entire capital as they had resolutely banded together. The Imperial Palace and the House of Arman were surreptitiously protecting the posters.

Additionally, the news was also spreading that the priests of the Temple who had lost their sacred powers had thrown out the true priests who still had theirs under false charges. But that was only the tip of the iceberg.

"I heard that the lady of the House of Arman made a contract with fairies! Real ones!"

"I thought fairies were just creatures in old wives' tales and legends?"

"Fairy stones are real, so of course fairies are, too!"

"I heard that the House of Rashahel were close to fairies."

"The problem is that the Temple was trying to extort the fairies!"

"My goodness, why?"

"They wanted to use the fairies' powers and trick people into believing that they had sacred powers!"

Those poor, fragile, and innocent fairies had burst into tears at the priests' terrifying advances. Or so the people heard.

That was why the House of Arman sent the Temple an official letter of protest.

"And that's not all! You know, the prophecy."

"Of course, of course!"

This news was significant. False prophecies.

There had been rumors and tidbits about the prophecies which had never blatantly surfaced due to the sensitivity of the matter. Now, however, people can openly speak about things they couldn't before.

"There's evidence."

A prophecy had been made by a true priest from the bloodline of the ancient high priest Varsha Brockel. As his name had emerged, so had the news about the true priests who had been thrown out of the Temple. The reason they had been kicked out was related to the prophecy.

"That means that it wasn't just once or twice that the Temple falsified prophecies!"

The Temple filled their own pockets and bellies with gold by declaring whatever they saw fit as the will of a god. Any priest who criticized them had been expelled.

"They weren't priests! They were pigs!"

All those issues emerged at once, but that was only the tip of the iceberg. There was also evidence proving that the culprit of every cruel massacre was not the tyrant but, shockingly, the Temple!

The Imperial Palace sent out a notice for the people who felt doubtful about the sudden barrage of information.

"His Imperial Majesty had allowed the Temple the opportunity to right its wrongs and corruptions, but its actions only became viler as time passed. The Temple threatened not only the Imperial Palace, but also His Majesty's fiancée, Lady Scarlett of the House of Arman. Owing to the verity that there had already been an attempt on her life once before, His Majesty had no choice but to abandon his hope for the Temple."

An assassination attempt! How unbelievable that the Temple would go that far! The people of the empire were in shock.

And the last living heir of the House of Masiar had also been killed because of the Temple.

Of course, Glenn had to be pronounced dead because he had turned into a fairy, and his "death" was also used in this way.

But that wasn't the end of the revelations of the Temple's despotism.

"Not only that, but the Temple had also pressured the emperor to end his relationship with Lady Scarlett and threatened to designate the Imperial Palace and the House of Arman as heretics if he did not."

That wasn't the work of a Temple; it was the work of criminals. The people were flabbergasted.

All this information burst out because the Temple

was no longer under the protection of the emperor, not to mention there was clear evidence to back it all up. The citizens of the empire began to despise the Temple. Their hearts were no longer devoted to it—nobles and commoners alike.

It was almost ridiculous how quickly everything had progressed, but it was also to be expected. Everything that the people had been holding inside had finally exploded. The tyrant's bad name transferred to the Temple instead, and with that trigger, the victims of the Temple had stepped up on their own. Most of the capital's citizens had turned their backs on the Temple the moment the news had spread, and the same was happening all over the continent.

It was truly a week of chaos.

Many clerics of the Temple frequently escaped in the dead of night. From their own mouths, additional information spread that the merciless Temple didn't even pay them any expenses for food.

"The Temple's reputation is plummeting into the depths of the earth just as we had planned," Count Ruman exclaimed excitedly, a delighted grin plastered on his face.

"We should have used this method earlier!"

Fighting by means of public opinion. It was an approach they couldn't have taken under normal circumstances because it required cornering the Temple from every angle.

However, they had to act before the Temple declared them heretics, and they had gathered more than enough palpable evidence for the people to see.

They said it was the lady of the House of Arman's idea, didn't they?

She was the perfect match for the emperor.

Of course, this was only possible because they had proof that the Temple was working with the dark wizards, so they were able to expose everything they had without worrying about the repercussions. They were prepared to bring everything to an end.

"We'll be able to end them once and for all! Mwahaha!" A sinister laugh escaped Count Ruman's lips.

Isar and the elders, who were at the palace with him, gave him slightly disapproving looks.

Yes, it's all a good thing.

But the chilling fact was that everything happened all over the continent at almost the same time. It was shocking enough that Isar and the elders wondered why in the world the emperor hadn't united the entire continent under his reign.

If anyone could do it, he could!

With those thoughts in mind, Isar and the elders began praising him to the best of their abilities.

"His Majesty's power is astounding!"

"We don't even need to use the magic of the House of Arman."

"Hmph, I can't help but acknowledge the excellence of the lies."

"Is it certain that those ass—I mean, those priests colluded with dark wizards? My..."

"Curse those vermin! In any case, good work."

Count Ruman smiled delicately. "Oh, we didn't lie! We merely embellished the incidents a tad bit."

"Yes, yes, of course you did."

The count was supposedly a timid crybaby, but he seemed overjoyed as he spent generous amounts of money and personnel to undertake this job.

And look at him, even now. No sign of modesty.

But that was fine. Honestly, the elders and Isar were delighted.

"Anyhow, now is not the time to toast our victory."

Isar tilted his head at Count Ruman's cryptic words. "Is there something else?"

The count grinned and pointed to the communication crystal, and Charlemagne's voice came out of it.

"We found a passageway that connects the temple to the dark wizards' headquarters. We'll be in touch once we deal with it."

"I suppose the next time you contact us, it will all be over, Your Majesty."

"That's right."

"To think you went to tear down the place yourself…"

Had the commander heard, he would have screamed and shouted to be taken along. How was it that the chancellor was at the best place to be right now? It was such a shame. Of course, the count wasn't the only one who felt that way.

"What is His Majesty planning to demolish?"

Technically, the emperor hadn't said anything about "demolishing" anything.

"Is our lord of the house with him? Then we should also…"

Two elders of Arman were slyly trying to squeeze into the party that had gone to the temple.

"Ahem…"

"Oh, and I do have several small golems… Ahem, ahem."

No, four elders.

Count Ruman chuckled for a moment and turned to Isar, who was reacting relatively normally to Charlemagne's words.

"Lord Isar."

Isar didn't answer immediately. He was staring at the crystal ball, where fairy fire was melting down some unknown part of the temple, and Scarlett was poking a priest who was blocking a doorway in the butt with an arrow made from her sacred power.

"Lord Isar? Oh dear… Lady Scarlett is quite…"

Count Ruman also saw what Lady Scarlett was doing and seemed to be unable to keep talking.

Scarlett… why his butt, of all places?

The crystal ball was unnecessarily large and had ultra-high definition.

"It appears there is no need for you to worry about Lady Arman, Lord Isar."

"Worry?" *Why would I worry about Scarlett?* He was so embarrassed that he wanted to run away. He would rather go home and talk to the duchess for thirty minutes than watch whatever *that* was in person.

Isar turned to the count with a grimace. "Yes, it looks like she can handle herself."

He noticed that there were now four fairies as well. He thought one of them looked like someone he knew, but it was probably his imagination. *Right?*

Isar almost felt stupid for being worried about Scarlett.

"Well then, you should go wait at the estate, Lord Isar. Based on our experience, we don't know what the Temple will do in retribution. Elders, you should go with him."

"Yes, then I shall take my leave." Unlike the elders, who seemed sorry to leave, Isar practically ran out of the office.

Count Ruman watched Isar run out of his office, slightly bewildered, and then turned around to look at the crystal ball and clamped his mouth shut.

Lady Scarlett kissed Emperor Charlemagne and then shouted at the high priest, who was blocking the doorway, "We feel really bad that you don't know what love is!"

Clerics can't get married. It's not that he won't, but that he couldn't.

They did an outstanding job stabbing at the high priest's sore spot. Even as the count's lips twitched at the sight, a thought crossed his mind.

He understood Isar's feelings when he ran away without watching any further.

CHAPTER
ONE HUNDRED AND FORTY

The week passed by quickly. No one had expected to be so busy, but things had become urgent because of Baba's words.

"Two gods have vanished."

Baba had said this on the way back to the capital. Our party halted at his dazed voice.

"What are you talking about?" the chancellor asked listlessly. "I thought you brought the book back easily."

Baba had returned to the group with the book that held the holy objects. The first thing he told us when he rejoined our party was that two of the gods had disappeared.

"The two dark wizards have taken two of the holy objects."

"Then, why did you say 'gods' and not 'holy objects'?"

"Because it means the same thing," Baba said in his hazy voice. He looked at me and Charlemagne, who were frowning. "What should we do?"

"What do you mean, what should we do? You must give us an explanation." I tried to sound intimidating, and the corners of Baba's mouth lowered.

"The holy objects are the last vestiges of the gods. They can be used to wake up the slumbering gods, but two of the objects were taken."

"I see."

"I have enough power to feel the presence of the sleeping gods, but I can't feel those two."

"What happened with the dark wizards who stole the book?" Charlemagne asked after listening quietly.

Baba tilted his head. "There weren't any dark wizards."

"Then, where did you retrieve the book from?"

"Well, the book just appeared at the place I called it from. It must have come to me when the person who stole it wasn't watching."

No wonder he came back so fast.

"What do you mean there weren't any dark wizards?" I asked.

"I remember what their manas felt like, but they didn't seem to have touched the book in days."

"And?"

"And calling the book to me is only possible if I'm somewhere near it. But I couldn't feel the dark wizards' presence anywhere nearby, no matter how I searched."

After a thoughtful grunt, I asked him another question.

"What if they went far away after they left the book where it was?"

"Maybe," Baba said. He didn't sound convinced. "But it bothers me that the holy objects disappeared."

"Hmm."

From what I had heard, the dark wizards who stole the book were Cheryl Diel and the weakest dark wizard.

It's ridiculous that this punk Baba already knew that Cheryl Diel was a dark wizard.

A strange feeling flitted through my chest.

"Ah!"

"Lett!" Charlemagne immediately held me up, as I staggered, holding my chest. "What's wrong?"

"Oh, uh..." Leaning dazedly on him, I pursued the feeling. "It feels as if mana had forcefully disappeared from me."

At my murmur, everyone gathered around and looked at me with concern.

"Lettie! Lettiiieee! Are you okay?"

"Sister! Dis one knows haw to heal. Do sumting! Now! Fast!"

"I-I will! I was gonna do it! You... you mean baby!"

"Ya! I'm mean. Yoor a slowpoke."

"Wah!"

I blinked as I heard the voices of Glenn, who was berating

Nell, and Nell, who was whining tearfully as Glenn pulled at his cheeks.

I was starting to understand.

"The power I planted."

"Hmm?"

I quickly began speaking before Nell started crying again. "A while ago, I saw someone who looked like the Cheryl from my prophetic dreams."

"Someone who looked like her?" No. 1 asked.

I nodded. "Yes. She was different from the person we saw recently, though her eyes were red. But I still got an uneasy feeling, so I planted a bit of the power from my holy object inside her."

"I think I know who you're talking about."

"You do? Hmm…"

"But why? What about that power?"

"It's gone."

I was sure the woman I'd seen then was Cheryl Diel, which meant that Cheryl Diel, a dark wizard, had intentionally approached Charlemagne in the novel.

"What kind of garbage… Anyway, Baba, can you trace Cheryl Diel?"

"Hmm. It will take about a day as she isn't close by. But I can't feel the holy object of infatuation that she took, either."

"Infatuation. Ugh, makes sense." I hugged Charlemagne tightly and mentally cursed out Cheryl in his arms. I felt much better after a bucketload of swearing.

I stepped away from him, feeling refreshed, and saw Charlemagne staring at me. His expression turned peculiar when our eyes met, and he turned his face to the side, covering his mouth. However, I noticed that he was actually laughing. I grinned as I poked his ribs lightly. Then, we immediately turned back to face the others, who were scowling at us.

"Let's think about this as we move."

"Whatever," Baba said. He sounded particularly sulky.

By the time we arrived at the capital, we had all come to a conclusion: the two holy objects must have been sacrificed for the descent of the devil.

"What's the dark wizard's name? The one who is to be the Descended?"

"He probably doesn't have one, especially if he's the Descended. The god that takes over his body will create a name he likes."

"You know so much," I said smiling, and Baba rolled his pink eyes shiftily.

"I-I don't know everything."

"We can't linger here. Shouldn't we hurry?" No. 2 piped up—his voice downcast.

"If the holy objects were used to aid the descent, then either the devil's seal has been broken or is starting to break, is that right?"

"He's right!" No. 3 agreed, her face pale.

And so, he was. That was why we decided to stop by the temple first.

"This means it will take us some time before we'll be able to use the holy objects, even if we manage to bring them out of the book," Baba commented sadly.

Once we brought the objects out of the book, we would need to find people who could use their powers until the sleeping gods inside them awoke. But if the seal was already starting to break...

"Ugh. I thought only the heirs of the gods could be used as sacrifices."

"Yes, for the devil's absolute advent. And for the seal to be completely broken, I think?"

"What happens when holy objects are sacrificed?"

"Not even a quarter of its powers will be released. That's why..." Baba's voice trailed off.

That's why his scheme was to get me and Charlemagne to make our move is probably what he wanted to say!

"But now that two holy objects have been sacrificed..."

"It doesn't matter. We know where their base is, and we

have evidence that it's connected to the Temple. We'll go in and crush them." Charlemagne's voice was cold.

The chancellor and the spies nodded as if to say, "*Of course, you would.*"

Just then, the voice of a god that only I could hear echoed in my mind.

– *Child. My child.*

It was a peaceful and gentle voice.

"W-who?"

"Lett? Oh," Charlemagne paused, and his face hardened. He appeared to be experiencing the same thing, although I wasn't sure if he heard the same voice.

– *You do not have to reply. There is no time, so simply listen to my words.*

I was certain that this was the voice of the Goddess of Fire. Had she woken up?

– *The God of the Sun and I have pondered this matter together, but the devil's presence is getting perturbingly stronger. We no longer have the luxury of finding a different way.*

What did she mean?

– *Either you or Kalior shall be sacrificed this time,* the voice continued sorrowfully. *He did not want me to tell you, but I believe that I must.*

The goddess fell silent for a moment.

– You must choose. However, if you choose to be sacrificed...

I stood there with my lips slightly parted.

– Your soul can be sent back to Korea.

"What does that mean?" I murmured into the air before me. The chancellor, the spies, and the fairies shuffled around confusedly, but I couldn't hear what they were saying.

Back to Korea? That means...

– Your soul was originally from this world.

"Huh?"

– It was split in two, and one half was sent to a different world, but this is your homeland, child of Arman.

I suddenly remembered Scarlett Arman, the child who didn't die despite having both Arman and Rashahel blood.

– Your mother made it possible. I only know through reading the traces, but even with traces, I can reach the place you were sent to.

The Goddess of Fire said that she, along with the God of the Moon, would help me. She told me to pierce the Descended's heart with a blade myself. Then, at the same time, I would become the sacrifice, the seal would break, and the Descended would die when he was most vulnerable.

And at that moment, my soul would be sent back.

– You found the place where you should be, and you must now find the entrance. Though you do not have much time, call to

me once you have made your choice.

"Uhm..."

– The important thing is to make sure you annul the engagement before you do so, because you are tied together as one through a magical contract. The contract will be destroyed if you express your intentions. That is the only way to keep the child of Kalior from getting hurt. I am sorry to tell you this.

Well, this is an ultimatum.

I settled my emotions, allowing myself only a moment to be surprised, and answered my goddess grudgingly. "I see. Okay."

My eyes met Charlemagne's. His expression was odd as well.

"What did your god say?"

"The Descended is in the temple."

"We really don't have time to hand out and utilize the holy objects, huh?"

Two days later, we searched every corner of the temple and then determined where we needed to break through. It was a tight schedule.

I still haven't made up my mind about the sacrifice, though.

Right now, I focused on the task at hand. We needed to

lose the clerics while Baba carefully opened the entrance to where the Descended was.

I kissed Charlemagne. "We feel really bad that you don't know what love is!" I shouted. The high priest looked highly affronted.

And right at that moment, I made up my mind.

I will make him dump me for sure this time.

CHAPTER
ONE HUNDRED AND FORTY-ONE

The dark water swelled with light splashing noises, followed by the roar of a waterfall. The sound of water intensified as it echoed from far away.

In a pitch-black space, there was a single area where the light shined brightly. Someone floated in the mysterious cave-like area that was as nebulous as outer space.

His entire body was black, and he had long, black hair which flowed like water. From a distance, it was more bizarre than beautiful.

An unknown amount of time had passed, and the sound of water began to diminish.

And then...

He opened his eyes. They were golden and they glowed faintly.

"Hmm."

A dark smile twisted his lips. He had just done something forbidden. Now, there was no one left in this world to welcome the god he served, because he had absorbed all their life energy.

"They should be honored."

The dead dark wizards were probably overjoyed. They certainly supported their beloved master in his descent, for which they had waited for so long.

Even though none of them smiled.

But what was he to do even if they weren't happy? It was all meant to happen in the first place.

The silent dark wizard contemplated the twisting souls that were packed inside him. Even though he had used enough of them to transport the headquarters to a different world, the power of the souls still overflowed within him.

The devil wasn't only counting on sacrificing the three houses. Had they brought the sacrifices from the houses of the dead gods, none of the dark wizards would have needed to die, but the devil had a secondary plan in case they failed.

Of course, I was the only one who knew.

Only he, who had been chosen as the Descended, had been privy to every plan his master made.

The slumbering gods could awaken through their holy objects and retain a physical form. But because the devil could not lay a hand on those objects, he had to gain a physical form before they did.

"Even if it is not perfect."

The splashing sound of a body standing up from within the water reverberated around the space.

"It is better than I expected."

He had taken other sacrifices because they had failed to present him with the three heirs. The dark wizards were shunned in this world because they served the devil. That was why they were the only ones who could tear through his seal, albeit feebly. The devil had generously shared his power with them, and now...

They had fully served their purpose.

"Perhaps it is due to the unexpected gain."

The state of his body was better than he had anticipated because Cheryl Diel and the weakest wizard had become the owners of holy objects.

It did not matter which objects they had held, since those objects had become part of the sacrifice.

"But..."

It wasn't all for the better. There was a penalty. He was supposed to have one full year. That was the amount of time he should've had to obtain a sacrifice.

"Now I only have three days."

He had to get his hands on a sacrifice in three days for his descent to be complete. He thought of the possible options.

Charlemagne Kalior.

Isar Arman.

And…

"Scarlett Arman. I desire her the most right now."

There were only outlines and no features on his pitch-black naked body, but his face was different. His beautiful face, whose age was impossible to determine, tilted slightly, and only his golden eyes shone.

While his face was certainly beautiful, it was also repulsive.

The voice, which was a mixture of masculine and feminine, became excited for the first time as it murmured Scarlett's name once more. She was a rare, rousing creature.

"A soul that split in two and then rejoined. Interesting for a human."

He couldn't understand how the divided soul had returned and merged, but no matter. The devil, who still thought of everything as a game, found her to be an appealing subject.

"She will be the next sacrifice." He felt a feeling close to certainty. If he took her soul, he would become perfect. "Time to get going."

If he didn't absorb a proper sacrifice in three days, he would be sealed again. He didn't know when the next opportunity would arise. There wasn't much time.

It's more fun this way, though.

The Descended's conscience still belonged to the silent dark wizard. He grinned and slashed his hand in the air. With a *clang*, the sound of the water moving stopped.

The space returned to an empty cave, and when it became bright again, it was empty once more.

I need to get dumped for sure this time.

I was surprised that magical contracts between humans still held up even if one party died, so now I have to deal with that first. Of course, I had no intention of ending this relationship immediately.

He's my man! I won't obediently just do as you gods tell me to.

The gods were making us humans clean up their mess. Jerks.

"Ahem."

But there was no reason for me to say that out loud. I resolutely made up my mind and called to the Goddess of Fire.

– Have you decided? The goddess reacted at once, sounding incredibly apologetic.

I pretended to be doleful as I asked her a question. *You said you needed the death of a god in order to kill a god, right?*

– Yes, but the only gods who can move right now are the heirs of the dead gods.

I spoke to her through my thoughts, just in case, and she understood me fine.

I stared at Charlemagne after I kissed him, and he looked like he wanted to kiss me again. It was a relief that he couldn't hear my goddess. His lips came closer.

I feel bad that I'm thinking about something else, but...

There was nothing for me to do. Half-immersed in a deep, slow second kiss, I spoke to my goddess.

How did you wake up?

– I woke up because an heir of the dead gods held my holy object. The God of the Sun used his power at the last minute to protect his last servant, Varsha Brockel, which explains why that god was already awake.

She was telling me things I didn't even ask.

Then, will everyone wake up if I touch them?

– Most of them have already awakened as a result of you and Kalior touching them. Perhaps if I lend you my power, the rest will wake up as well.

I liked that she was calmly telling me everything because she was apologetic.

– You mentioned that you wanted to give out the holy objects, did you not?

Yes, I did.

– Ah, you are concerned about the future. Thoughtful child, do not worry. Once you use all the sacred power that I pour into you and wake the sleeping gods, the holy objects will fly to find their rightful users.

Oh, really?

That wasn't what I had wanted to know, but it was helpful information. That was that, but...

Charlemagne! How long is he planning to kiss me for?

"W-wait."

"Okay."

As I took several deep breaths, he waited for a moment before smiling and drawing his lips closer to me.

Again? "You do remember where we are?" I whispered.

"Of course," he replied with a tinge of laughter. "Not that it matters."

True that. I gently closed my eyes. My mind was half-dazed because of his lips that devoured mine.

– Yes, well. If you use the power too much, you will become theirs, so you should be careful, but it should be useful for now. Hmm.

I could sense that she was a little put off.

– I shall have them attempt to fly to those who are close to you. Every member of your party that is here with you should be

able to receive one. The God of the Moon and I shall lend you our strength to do that.

Oh, nice.

"What! How dare you! What do you think you are doing in this sacred temple?!"

I glanced at the head priest, who was seething at us, and smirked.

Actions speak louder than words.

The high priest, who was grinding his teeth, suddenly felt Charlemagne's bloodlust, and peed himself in fear.

"E-Emperor! You must be insane!" That was all he could utter.

"I wish those two would be considerate toward us."

"Lord Baba, are you still clinging to false hope? We've all given up."

"You people have been chaste for all of thirty years, but me... Ugh..." Baba's voice trailed off. He was clearly a lot older than he looked.

Charlemagne and I finally parted lips. As I was enjoying the feeling that lingered from that long kiss, I briefly wondered how old Baba was. *I should ask him later.*

"Chaste? I'm far from being chaste. I'm temporarily single because I find my job entertaining."

"No. 1 isn't the only one! I might be a 'sickly lady' now,

but I'm quite popular in social circles when I attend, you know."

"Me too! It's not that I can't, but that I won't."

I didn't spare a glance at the spies quibbling with Baba. I only felt sorry for the chancellor.

"Damn it all."

Apparently the only one who had received a critical hit from Baba's comment, the chancellor leaned on the wall and slid to the ground. The fairies that I had casually left with him when Charlemagne and I began kissing started chattering to each other.

"This place feels disgusting!"

"Like they didn't clean!"

"Should we clean it for them?"

"Hmph... Dat butthoole emp'rer... do dat to my sister..."

Pretending not to hear Glenn's sour words, I smiled at the high priest as though nothing had happened. "All right, then."

Following the trail made by the items and structures that held the mark of Lycos, I determined that the entrance to the Descended's location had to be the door the high priest was doggedly blocking.

The storage room was closed off because one of the clerics had committed suicide, right?

Luckily for me, it just opened with a faint creak. The high priest jumped in surprise. Meanwhile, I turned to Charlemagne to call off the engagement, while simultaneously giving the Goddess of Fire a belated answer to her query.

"Charl, let's call off our engagement," I said.

The glinting eyes that were gazing at me started to blink slowly, and a moment later, his face completely froze.

CHAPTER ONE HUNDRED AND FORTY-TWO

Charlemagne was quiet for a bit before he opened his mouth to speak.

"Why?" Charlemagne asked me calmly. Surprisingly, his face was relaxed, and his lips pulled into a comforting smile. I felt that he was encouraging me to say whatever I wished. And as I watched his calm face, I finally realized something.

He loves me. And it might not be a fleeting feeling after all.

I didn't believe in love all that much, and I especially didn't believe that love could last forever. *Also, I'm not even his ideal type, so any love between us probably wouldn't last that long.*

Of course, I wasn't denying that there were deep and powerful emotions that drove people to die for others. But how would I know if a person felt that way toward me?

And it's not like I need to receive that kind of love anyway. Isn't it enough to be happy right at this moment?

Yeah, well, that's what romantic relationships are like.

Even I, who had been single my entire life, knew that.

That was why I thought it didn't matter. Or so I thought.

I began to think, *maybe his feelings are deeper and might last longer than I thought.*

Before I explained myself, I asked Charlemagne an unfair question. "Will you break up with me if I tell you the reason?"

He gave me a gentle smile. "I'm not sure," he said.

But then in a soft voice that gave me chills, he continued, "But probably not."

"Ah, you were basically saying, 'Let's hear it first,' right?"

"Even if you hate me…" he trailed off smiling. His smile was always so tender toward me. Then, the smile twisted slightly, and the violet eyes that I always praised as brilliant became dark.

"I probably won't be able to let you go," he said, softly caressing my cheek. I could feel a certain intensity coming from him, but at the same time, every movement was also filled with love. "That's how I feel, Lett."

Before I could feel more hurt from the strength of his feelings, I said playfully, "Wow, that's fascinating. I'm super scared of being hated by you."

"Yet, you would say something like that?"

"Well… you hate me now, don't you? I understand."

Charlemagne blinked, confused. Then, he laughed softly and sliced whatever was behind me with his sword.

"U-urgh!"

That's the high priest's voice. The moment the thought crossed my mind, the smell of blood washed over me.

Stopping me from turning around instinctively, Charlemagne asked me, "So, your reason?"

"Well..." I stood on my tiptoes to whisper quietly in his ear. "My goddess told me that our engagement contract is hindering the fight, so let's break it off for now and then get married when the fight's over."

At my words, Charlemagne shoved me back. He gripped my shoulders at arm's length as his eyes bore into my face.

I've never seen that face before.

I didn't know he could make such a flustered, angry, and ecstatic face. I let out a snort of laughter without meaning to, and his eyes became fiery.

– *Sweet child,* the Goddess of Fire whispered to me in a strangled voice. *Now the child of Kalior can also focus on the battle before him. I was worried how he would react when you said you wanted to break off the engagement. What a kind and wise child you are.*

Asshole gods, I thought to myself. *Just wait until I pull the rug out from under your feet. Sacrificing myself is not my style. I can't tell Charlemagne everything because I have to be careful with my own thoughts.*

No one was going to be sacrificed, including Baba, who, when no one was looking, had secretly sent me his blue bird with the book and fled the scene.

No one, except for gods.

Laughing insidiously to myself, I put my arms around Charlemagne as he pulled me into a tight embrace.

"What? Aren't you going to answer?" I asked him sullenly, and he let out a breath of laughter.

He kissed me on the side of my head, my forehead, and my lips. "I'm just overwhelmed. I love you, Scarlett."

A weird giggle slipped out of me. *Oh my god! He loves me! Bwahaha!* His warm lips landed lightly on my stupid grin.

"That's the perfect answer."

Our kiss continued, gradually becoming deeper, in the area where the high priest was dying in a pool of his own blood.

"How about you?"

"Hmm, me too."

Thus, we pledged our futures to one another.

"I love you, Charl."

The chancellor lifted his head as a frail hand tapped him on the shoulder.

"It. Is. Over."

It was Glenn who, though unreliable as a human being, was now more useful as a fairy. According to Glenn, the emperor was almost finished with his bizarre "stab and kiss" situation. The chancellor lowered his hands from his ears, relieved.

But then...

"I love you, Scarlett."

"I love you, too."

He heard the sappy words that he never wanted to hear other people say.

Glenn cackled wickedly at the chancellor as the man gave him a betrayed look.

Fairies can hear everything, even if we cover our ears!

He wanted the chancellor to suffer with him. How dare the chancellor try to escape on his own? That Varsha Brockel guy had sneakily run off somewhere, but...

He did say that seeing his friends act like that was torture, so I'll let him off the hook.

Glenn floated over to where the other three fairies were watching.

"Clover sick?"

"Angry? Why?"

"He's crying!"

Hmph, good. Glenn shook his little butt to express his tiny joy.

The spies muttered among themselves as the kiss went on and on.

"Have you cleared the west side?"

"Yes."

"And the east?"

"Yes. But they're still not done yet."

"Eek! Oh my!" No. 3 was the only one squealing in delight at the kissing scene before her.

No. 1 and 2 had worked their butts off to clear the entire temple. They had locked up all of the remaining clerics, separated the ones whose atrocities had been the worst, and submitted requests for trials, and the kiss was still going on!

The two were lost in their own world.

Of course, taking care of these things was their job, and the pair would be in the most danger once they stepped through that door, but still...

"The, uhh, the high priest is dying."

"Should we inform Count Ruman? We need to take him alive and put him on trial to clear our emperor's name."

"Should I go?"

"No, we need to stay here, and so do the dear fairies."

"Then, as I'm the most useless person here, I'll take *that* to the palace." The chancellor popped into the conversation, pointing at the high priest, and refusing to regard him as a human being.

No. 1 snickered at his feisty words and nodded. "I was going to tell you to hurry up and return home anyway."

He plopped the half-dead high priest, who was spilling blood, onto the chancellor's back. Normally, the chancellor would have screamed, but he quickly moved without complaining.

"Damn it! Damn it!" However, his resentful exclamations could be heard as he moved further away.

No. 1 determinedly resolved to find someone who would shower the chancellor with lots and lots of love.

Finally, a ray of light shone between Scarlett and Charlemagne as their contract was broken, even though nothing was actually going to change between them.

And so, the three fairies and three spies, as well as Scarlett and Charlemagne, stepped forward.

They headed toward the place where the final dark wizard—no, the Descended—was waiting.

Baba halted as he trudged along. He had left his blue bird with Scarlett, and he was planning on sharing his plans with his friends once their public display of affection was over.

There were only two reasons he'd left on his own: The God of the Sun, and the back door.

"I'll block the retreat if I lock this door, correct?"

The God of the Sun, who had already figured out where Scarlett and Charlemagne were heading, confirmed this.

– Yes. The Descended will not be able to leave this temple.

"Hmm."

– Though this place has been taken over by the servants of the devil, the building itself is still a temple. It has been a base for many priests over the ages. It has remained an important institution to this day even though it has been remodeled numerous times.

Among those institutions was one that was entangled with "providence," which was something even the devil couldn't do anything about.

"And you're certain this is the place?" Baba asked coldly. Even though his god hadn't known, there was no way Baba could speak nicely now when he had been led to believe that this world was fake all this time.

– I am! I told you I would help you with whatever I can. Trust me.

"If I get the feeling that something is wrong, I will never call on you again and I will live my life pretending that gods don't exist."

It was a bloodcurdling threat. The God of the Sun nodded sadly.

– *I understand.*

Baba used his god's power to block the only exit.

After a moment, he headed to where his friends were.

The place looked like a regular part of the temple.

"You are late."

The figure, pitch-black in its entirety, seemed to have amassed all the eeriness of the world. Only his eyes were brilliantly golden, while everything else was pitch black. He was beautiful and vile at the same time. He looked like a black tree, or the very embodiment of hell.

The being opened its mouth. "It was too boring to sit and wait, so I unleashed some of my minions on the capital. Have you seen them?"

Count Ruman was bewildered as he watched through the communication bead that Emperor Charlemagne was holding. He had no way of knowing beforehand, but he had expected something like this.

Scarlett spoke to her fairies. Glenn and Gill waved to Bell and Nell, who were flying away.

"It is useless to send those fairy younglings to help."

"Hmm, I'll have to kiss tons of fruit until my lips get swollen again."

It was the beginning of history's swiftest, yet most pointless war.

ONE HUNDRED AND FORTY-THREE

"Minions?"

"My demons and monsters. But they are far too beautiful to be called such."

At the elegant string of words, Charlemagne stopped asking questions and pointed his holy sword, Opere, at the dark being. He had to wrap things up quickly here and prevent a horrible massacre. Some of the fairies had gone outside to fight the minions, so they would buy him some time.

And Count Ruman will help them out, too.

Even if Charlemagne hadn't changed through the year inside the book, he still would have attempted to prevent a situation like this. His enemies had always been the dark wizards, not his innocent citizens.

"Oh." The communication bead he held shattered in his hand.

"The item you have seems quite bothersome."

The devil was probably talking about both the bead and Opere, but Opere couldn't be destroyed. It didn't matter, though; Count Ruman should have already understood the situation.

Peep! The blue bird, which had gone unnoticed so far, cried out. Scarlett, who had been silently observing the Descended, suddenly smiled. In that moment, images of what Baba had done for his allies appeared in her head, along with the message that he was going to join them soon. And that was not all.

I can see another video of what happened.

She saw the dark wizards that the devil had consumed, and the sight of Cheryl Diel being eaten.

That dark thing over there was the last enemy standing.

Good. How simple. Let's get started then, shall we?

Scarlett smirked as she murmured, as if she wanted him to hear her, "Fascinating. It's trying to talk when it looks like that."

The golden eyes that had been fixed on Opere shifted to look at her instead. Stifling Opere's humming, Charlemagne stood close to Scarlett.

"I cannot sense an inkling of respect for the gods within you, Scarlett Arman." But the Descended didn't seem too displeased. "That is why I am even more keen on you."

Charlemagne scowled as the Descended showed its interest in Scarlett. At that moment, he felt power flow into him from the ring on his finger.

"Charl, hold this."

"All right."

Not even sparing a glance toward the devil, Scarlett handed Charlemagne the book with the holy objects. "I have a proposal."

Charlemagne held the book tightly with his free hand.

"It will be worth listening to since you are both the children of gods. What do you say? Will you listen?"

Swoosh! With a pure ringing sound, the fairies cheered enthusiastically.

"Tsk. The power of the Goddess of Fire has no combat power. I don't understand why she is a great god."

The Descended prattled on even though no one answered or spoke to him. The truth was, he had to wait a little longer for his plan to work. Once his demons had massacred the humans and absorbed their life energy, he would be able to crush these children with overwhelming power. As such, he was passing the time in a leisurely manner.

But that didn't mean the atmosphere was relaxed. The Descended's voice, which was a blend of male and female, was chilling, and the spies nearby couldn't help but tense up. However, Scarlett and Charlemagne didn't seem too bothered. Neither were the fairies.

As the fairies looked on in fascination, Scarlett shouted in her mind: *More, more! Ugh, is this all you can do?!*

– B-but, I have never poured this much power before!

You're a great god, aren't you?

– My power is the power of healing, and my role was to show wanderers the way, which doesn't require that much power.

Her goddess sounded sulky, but Scarlett didn't care.

Didn't you hear what that thing just said?

The goddess tilted her head questioningly.

He said that your abilities were insignificant, without a smidge of attack power, and that he didn't know why you were a great god in the first place!

– H-he did not say my power was insignificant.

I didn't even respond because I thought you'd be upset!

– Did you really? What a kind child you are.

Scarlett pressed her goddess, whose voice sounded both pitiful and deeply moved. *Give it your all so he can't say any-thing like that ever again!*

Scarlett had given her the carrot, so it was time for the stick. With that logic, Scarlett vocalized her encouragements. "Come on, now! Let's go!"

– Fine! All that will happen is that I will sleep longer! Let's go!

Her goddess was more naive than she had expected. But, thanks to her goddess' gullibility, Scarlett's power exploded.

The blinding light was so bright that people outside of the temple could see it as well.

"Wh-what is she doing?" Baba, having rejoined their party again, stared at Scarlett, aghast. "If she does that, the gods...!"

They would be forced to wake up!

Baba knew that much power wouldn't harm Scarlett physically because her goddess had allowed it, but that wasn't the problem.

At this rate, all the objects will belong to Scarlett!

Because she was an Arman with Rashahel blood.

Normal people would have been sucked into the book and died with the holy objects, or failed to wake them at all, but Scarlett was different. Since she was the child of two gods, it was certain that every god was going to awaken.

The devil also knew this, but he simply observed her. "Why is she doing that? What is her goal?"

She wouldn't be able to use many of the powers. Not because it was predetermined but because there were different types of synergy between the gods. A person's body would break if they used the powers of the sun and moon gods at the same time, and their body would have shattered if they combined the sacred powers of fire and winter gale. Ignorantly harboring all the powers would do more harm than good.

What is she going to do with them all? Why does she think I kept them stored away?

Baba tried to approach Scarlett, but the Goddess of Fire's power was so strong that he couldn't even get close. All he could do was shout at Charlemagne, who was holding the book and his sword.

"Hey! Stop her!"

Charlemagne, however, didn't move a muscle. He simply glanced at his ring every now and then.

The ring is reacting to the light.

The God of the Moon was waking up. And slowly, softly, its power was heading toward the sacred power of fire.

The moon and fire, which are guides of the night, have great synergy with the God of Travelers. This thought rang in Charlemagne's head. Opere had already explained this to him, which was why he was standing still.

"Hehe!"

Also, Scarlett was enjoying herself.

But to Baba, who couldn't see either of their expressions, Scarlett seemed to be doing something extremely pointless and using up all her energy.

"How foolish," The devil sneered gracefully as he spoke in his eerie voice. "Cease this nonsense and listen to me. Would you two not want to take down this insignificant world with me and..."

He yearned to tempt them with his silver tongue and play with their lives. *Now that this boring game is almost over, I must at least secure my next bit of entertainment.*

But just as the thought crossed its mind, the Descended halted and cocked its head.

Pages from the book fluttered to the ground. Various holy objects began to emerge.

"Hmm."

Contempt welled in his eyes. Gathered in front of him were the gods who had tried to trick him, but instead had fallen into a trap themselves. They looked ridiculous.

To the naked eye, the holy objects looked like regular objects, but in reality, they acted as houses for the sleeping gods.

Seeing as their houses are so small, their powers must have decreased as well.

They were gods who couldn't even hurt humans, so it would probably take them a long time to fully recover.

This game was bound to end with his victory.

As the devil stood there sneering, a few of the holy objects flew through the ominous air and the tempest of the fire's sacred power and vanished. Some went to the fairies and the spies, and others soared out of the temple.

There were still many left, so no one except for Scarlett, Charlemagne, and the fairies realized that some holy objects had disappeared.

The fairies—both inside and outside of the temple—looked at the holy objects, which were in powder form, in confusion as they approached them. As did Isar, who was on his way back home and had gotten stranded along with Lady Fletta.

And Lady Fletta, who, until she ran into Isar, had been wandering around crying because she couldn't control the strange, superhuman strength in her right hand.

Count Ruman and the chancellor, who were at the palace; the Commander of the Knights; the four elders, who were following Isar; and the duchess, who was at the Arman estate, also experienced the same thing.

A holy object also found its way to the seer in the dungeons.

All those people had spent much time with both Scarlett and Charlemagne, which had strengthened them as vessels, and the holy objects had gone to search for them.

And soon, the holy objects gave them new powers.

With that, the sacred light fulfilled its duties and began to diminish, and the holy objects that had been left behind revealed their forms more clearly.

Scarlett gathered the objects into her arms. When Charlemagne was about to help, she shook her head and sent him a wordless hint instead. Then, she turned to the Descended, who was disparaging the gods that had just awoken.

"Me, use them? Hmph. Who even said that?"

She whispered tenderly to the objects. At once, the holy objects began to twitch, as if they were surprised.

The devil tilted his head. "Why did you wake them if you are not going to use them? Amusing child, you are more entertaining than those gods."

Suddenly, a crack then appeared on the Descended's solid body. It hadn't noticed and continued talking.

"That is why I want you petty humans to... Hmm?"

Murky blue blood began seeping through the crack.

Undiscovered, Charlemagne had moved behind the Descended's shoulder.

Opere shouted in anger, "I cut off a god's words!" Though the voice was flustered, it was genuinely excited.

"Kalior! Don't people usually listen to what the villain has to say until the end? I was keeping to that unspoken rule, but my, oh my!"

Opere screamed with a mixture of fear and delight as it shivered. "Oh, this feels so good! Wahahaha!"

Once the devil gazed vacantly at its own spurting blood and flinched, Charlemagne proceeded to attack him once again.

Just as she had signaled him to.

CHAPTER ONE HUNDRED AND FORTY-FOUR

What I had whispered to the gods earlier was this:

"Considering the dead gods, the world on the other side of the Mirror, the slumbering gods, and the descent of a god, I'm guessing you absolutely need physical bodies. And not just physical bodies, but an actual world."

It seemed that they needed vessels, to be precise. My goddess had mentioned something about it when she was talking to me about sacrifices.

"Then, are these holy objects, or are these gods?"

I recalled how the objects had twitched at my question, like I had hit the nail right on the head.

If that's the case...

I organized my thoughts, realizing that was absolutely the case. If I was the only one who could die, it was due to a difference between me and the gods. The main distinction lay in our vessels. Sacred powers could only be harnessed by gods when contained within a vessel. Such gods were called awakened gods, but, as a consequence, they could die.

The devil also did a whole bunch of different things while he was contained, but the gods only tried to kill him after *his descent.*

This had to be the same for any god, no matter how powerful they were. The gods most likely wouldn't have died even if they awoke in the fake world on the other side of the Mirror.

And that was what the devil was aiming for if a god had to die to kill another god. Thus, the devil can't be killed even if the other gods wake up.

But things were different now.

Of course, the devil already knew that. He was probably nervous now that the holy objects had entered the real world.

"Hmm."

However, I couldn't find an inkling of apprehension in him.

So, the devil thinks the other gods waking up is meaningless, does he? Then, that means there's something else that's needed to kill a god.

That's why I had asked Charlemagne—to stall him.

Without taking my eyes off the devil, I desperately racked my brain. What was it? Why wasn't the devil uneasy despite seeing that all the holy objects had woken up? What else was needed?

I need to fully awaken all the holy objects. Only then could I finish my plan.

Just then, I heard giggles from the area that several holy objects had flown to in powdered form.

"Huh? What dis?"

"Kyahaha!"

Glenn and Gill started flapping their wings, their faces flushed.

"What's wrong?"

"D-dis is stwange!"

And with those words, their bodies began to grow.

"Ugh!"

Charlemagne let out a short grunt, and the Descended ground his teeth. In that next moment, the two fairies changed into young boys as tall as my waist.

"Woah."

"Wow! Yay!"

The two grown fairies blinked in surprise and then cheered. They grinned as they looked at each other, and then winked at me telling me not to worry. In the blink of an eye, they zoomed to where Charlemagne was. They joined him in overwhelming the Descended, and the Descended looked agitated for the first time.

"Geugh!" He let out a huge groan. But after a few attacks, he flashed his eyes, which had turned a deeper gold, and began to fill the air with a dark smog.

Poison!

Everything that the smog touched was rotting black.

"This way, Lady Scarlett!"

As I used the power of the goddess to protect myself and the other holy objects, No. 1 pulled me back, looking like he was in pain. When I turned around, I saw that all three of the spies had cold sweat raining down their faces.

"What's wrong?"

"This," No. 1 replied curtly as he bit his lip.

This?

He held out his arm with great difficulty, and I saw that a tattoo had been branded into his arm. No. 3 had red ruby earrings, and No. 2 had gloves.

"Are those holy objects?"

Unable to speak, No. 1 nodded faintly, and the corners of his ever-smiling lips trembled. He swallowed hard before attempting to speak again. "It's not bad, but I think we need some time, Lady Scarlett."

"I see."

The fairies had accepted the objects easily, but it seemed that humans needed more time. *Why?*

Baba, who had been glaring at the holy object that had flown to him, said out loud, in response to my unasked question, "It's because of the difference in the power of their souls. Human vessels aren't the same as fairies. Still, it's amazing they're able to use some of their power in that state. But those fairies..."

He glanced at me and the fairies. "All of them appear to be fairy kings. I didn't know that even Glenn had the potential to be a fairy king, though."

"Fairy kings?" *My babies are kings?*

"The origin of all fairies—No! Seriously! Stop! I said no! One is troubling enough as it is! Just shut up." Baba suddenly stopped talking to me and started yelling in an annoyed voice tinged with anxiety.

"Who are you talking to?"

"This holy object! It keeps begging me to accept it, but it's not even compatible with me. Do I look like an idiot?"

"But your soul is not really human, right? It probably isn't compatible."

Baba twitched at my words. "I am human... I'm just a bit different. But not as much as you are. To be honest, I think I know the reason why those holy objects are docilely staying by your side. Though you won't be able to use them all because of compatibility." He muttered the last sentence very quietly, but I could still hear him.

As I watched Charlemagne and the fairies fight against the Descended, I came to a conclusion.

I knew what had to be sacrificed.

I grinned, and Baba and the spies gave me nervous looks.

– *Child,* the Goddess of Fire called. *The holy objects say they will lend you their power. Keep pushing the devil into a corner, and once they deal with all the minions outside, you can charge at him.*

You'll tell me when I must die?

– *Yes... Oh kind child, I am sorry.*

You should be. And you should pay the price if you're so sorry! Hiding my true thoughts, I smiled brightly at the goddess.

Then, I'll wait until the moment the sacrifice is needed.

– *All right...*

Oh, and...

I saw that all the objects were things I could put on my body—a tattoo, a hairpin, a flower, a wooden doll, and so on.

All these gods can awaken if I wear the holy objects, right? I asked my goddess as I put all of them on me. I loosely put them on my arm, so I could shake them off whenever I wanted.

– *Yes. Since your soul is divided, they decided to use the half that is fading away. If we use your half, then you will not have enough strength to travel to the other world.*

Oh, nice. I had wanted to ask them to do that, but now I didn't have to.

As I nodded, the powers of the holy objects began to seep into me. At the same time, a roar of voices expressing their thanks and relief filled my ears. I listened quietly, solemnly regarding the battle before me.

I didn't know how much time had passed before the Goddess of Fire spoke again.

– It is almost time. The humans outside are highly competent.

This world was truly the real world...

Lady Fletta screamed, "Kyaaa! What are these things? Gross! Go away!"

Isar, who was suddenly stuck with a lady that he had never spoken to before, knitted his brows unconsciously. The noble lady's voice was so loud that it muffled the growls of the demons around them.

Who the hell is this lady? From what he had heard briefly earlier, her holy object had intensified her most probable potential. *But why is her fist like that?*

Cold sweat beaded on Isar's forehead as he remembered the lady bawling about how only her voice was going to be intensified.

But her potential was superhuman strength!

He could see the elders, who were protecting a group of

people from afar, staring at her with their mouths open.

One punch from her fist could kill someone.

Trying his best to ignore her, Isar focused on his own weapon. The azure-colored whip that he was whirling around was protecting the people around him. It looked like it had electricity flowing through it and didn't create a horrible scene, but the lady...

"Boohoohoo! Argh! Kyaaa!"

Pow! Pow! Pow!

Isar and the people who were being protected were thinking the same thing: *She seems stronger than those demons.*

Her fist is scarier than the whip.

Oh wow, that sound when the demons explode...

Gasp!

Demons flew into the air around Lady Fletta as she punched them fiercely, screaming about how scared she was. The demons didn't even get a chance to scream as they exploded. The way she was punching had gone beyond making people feel safe, and now it was sending chills down everyone's spine.

Luckily, these incidents were only happening at the Arman estate and the palace in the capital for now. But according to Baba, the Descended was planning on sending out his demons further once they finished destroying those two areas.

"I just received word through the communication bead," Count Ruman informed the others around the capital.

They had to kill all the demons.

"We need to destroy the demons before they spread to the rest of the continent."

Thinking that it was a relief that he didn't have to move around, Isar focused on his whip once again. Though Isar and the others didn't know it, the holy objects that had flown to the capital were the gods who wanted to protect humans.

They didn't give any regard to the child of Arman, who was to be sacrificed, and had gone to find ways to help them stay in this real world. They were planning to sacrifice themselves if needed. The souls of those who had been close to Arman and Kalior had been influenced far more than they had expected.

These souls are quite solid.

A few had difficulties like the spies, but even so, it was a smooth process.

Thank heavens more demons aren't appearing.

We can wipe them all out.

After some time, every demon of the early phase was obliterated.

Back at the temple, the Goddess of Fire shouted, *Now, child! Aim for his heart before he has the chance to release more demons! He will stab you, and if you let my power explode when he does, the devil will start to die.*

A suicide mission, ha. Just you wait. Scarlett dashed forward and aimed for the devil.

– Hold yourself together until he's completely dead. You have two halves of one soul, so you must hold out until both halves have been pierced and he swallows you.

Then, locking eyes with Charlemagne's wide ones, Scarlett lunged at the devil. The Descended sensed an ominous threat and whirled his arm.

"Lett!"

"Gaaah!" Scarlett let herself be pierced by the arm that shot out, and then shoved every single holy object that had been dangling from her arm into the mouth that gaped open to swallow her.

– Ch-child? What in the world...! Why—Argh!

Every holy object—no, every god—that hadn't become the possession of someone else tumbled into the Descended's throat, and Scarlett released the explosive power of the Goddess of Fire.

The sacred power scorched the other powers, and it burned even more ferociously as it clashed with the powers it was incompatible with.

The power flared silently, engulfing everything—everything except humans.

Watching the combustion of light, Charlemagne and Scarlett grinned at each other.

They were victorious.

CHAPTER
ONE HUNDRED AND FORTY-FIVE

Baba froze, dumbfounded, as the holy objects he had protected his entire life burned away. He was the only one who was speechless.

"I-is it over?" No. 1 stammered, unlike his usual self, and No. 2 and No. 3 passionately hugged each other.

Eh? What the...?

Leaving behind No. 1, who was staring at the other two in surprise, Glenn and Gill dashed over to me. *Woosh!*

"Sister! You're a genius!"

"Kya! Lettie, you're amazing!"

Honestly, Charlemagne and the fairies had done all the hard work.

"Me? I'm amazing?" I giggled as I looked at Charlemagne. "I guess the last blow is the most important hit."

Charlemagne approached me, looking more disheveled than I had ever seen him. "It's unfortunate that the temple didn't explode, though." Still, even as he said that, he looked far more refreshed than he had ever been.

I held back the laughter that was threatening to burst out. "Is it really over?"

"Most likely, thanks to you," he responded with a faint smile, and he lifted me into his arms. "Get some rest, Lett."

Such a tender voice.

I relaxed and leaned into him. "How did you know? I'm a bit sleepy."

"Because I've seen you like this many times before."

"Oh yeah..."

Baba looked over at me and let out a heavy sigh, apparently having returned to his senses. He approached us, frowning furiously. "Be careful when you move her. The smallest impact could put her in danger."

Charlemagne nodded wordlessly.

My vision was blurry as I slipped in and out of consciousness. There was a reason I was so exhausted. The Goddess of Fire hadn't given me permission to use her power at the last moment. *Well, of course she didn't.*

But I could still feel her power, so it seemed that only the gods that were trapped in their holy objects had been sacrificed. The silver lining was that the goddess couldn't stop me from using her power, so the connection hadn't been severed.

Anyway, that was probably why I wasn't in the best

condition at the moment.

"It would be nice if you could support me while you hold her. My head hurts because my god keeps screaming at me."

I guess his god has the strength to speak. I wasn't sure if mine couldn't or wouldn't.

"You walk on your own."

"Hmph."

The two fairies—no, fairy kings—called to me with trembling voices.

"S-sister?"

"Lettieee!"

I rubbed their heads and then fell into a deep sleep.

I don't know what's going to happen from now on. But the world won't get destroyed since this is the real one, right?

That's all that matters. I'll think about other stuff later.

I felt reassured as I lay in Charlemagne's warm and peaceful arms.

A week passed. I opened my eyes after five days, and the power of the Goddess of Fire was still inside me. She still wouldn't talk to me, though.

Once I'd spent a few days resting my body, I headed back to the Arman estate. A part of the mansion had collapsed during the attack, but luckily, the main area that housed people hadn't been touched.

"It's because of the m-madam's sacred power."

When I asked, with trembling lips, what had happened, Isar answered flatly, "The demons used sound attacks, but her holy object had the power to erase sound."

"So... soundproofing."

"Yeah."

Just as I was about to say that it was a relief that such a useless power existed, we heard a voice.

"I am quite satisfied with it," the duchess, who had silently opened the door to my room, commented elegantly.

"Welcome, Duchess."

Isar remained silent, so I welcomed her as enthusiastically as I could. She stared at me and then clicked her tongue and nodded.

"Scarlett," she said in a cold voice, "You are the lord of the House of Arman. You should know better and protect your own body, not act like a fool."

"The duchess is right."

It was the first time I had seen the mother and her son agree.

I grinned. "But the seal of the lord of the house did its job well."

"The seal?"

"What?" *Oh, I forgot to tell them.* I tapped my chest. "I found the power that protects the lord of the house. I almost died in the end, but this protected me."

And I hadn't lost consciousness because my mind synchronized with my fairy kings.

The two watched me, speechless, and then frowned in the exact same way.

"So, you're saying..."

"...you almost died?"

What happened between them? Why are they finishing each other's sentences?

I stared at them, smiling awkwardly, and they both sighed at the same time.

"Scarlett," said the duchess.

"Yes?"

"I said I would teach you something that only I knew."

"Yes, you did."

"But I never got the chance to."

"Y-yes."

"Do you have time now?"

I nodded. Isar looked displeased, but he didn't stop the duchess. It was unsettling.

The duchess said, with her usual cold expression, "I

shall teach you everything in great detail."

"Teach me what?"

"About the duties of the lord of the house, an overview of what that entails, and the history of this house. There are things you must learn that are not written in books."

But... that's not what I wanted to learn from you! I wanted to learn what I needed to live on my own when I go out on a journey.

Before I could voice my thoughts, however, the duchess curled her lips elegantly and whipped around and out of the room.

"You said you wanted to learn something from that perfectionist? You really dug your own grave, didn't you?" Isar commented sarcastically.

I stared at him and called Glenn with my mind.

"Sister, did you call for me?" Glenn appeared in my room. He was as big as a human now that he was a fairy king, but he still looked like a child.

"I did."

"That's the jerk, right?" Isar asked.

"Yup. You've heard, haven't you? Our little Glenn is now a fairy king. Say hi."

Glenn was enough to get under Isar's skin.

"I'll accept your greeting because my sister wants me to." Glenn smiled like an angel as he spoke to Isar. Isar opened and closed his mouth like a fish for a while before he dashed out of the room, saying he would see me later.

He's probably running to the elders.

The four elders had also been chosen by holy objects, and they'd become closer to Isar because of it. Perhaps it was because they had fought side by side.

No, that doesn't explain Lady Peridot Fletta.

It was fascinating to me that the noble lady had fallen for Isar. The elders made fun of him about it often, and that was why he had escaped to my room in the first place. But seeing as he'd rushed back to them...

"He must have not wanted to greet you."

"I'll go find him later. But about Bell..."

I listened to what Glenn had to say and enjoyed my last day of rest. The next day, I roughly inspected the estate before I headed to the palace.

To where Charlemagne was waiting.

The God of the Sun yelled at Baba for a while before he moved to a place where Baba couldn't hear him.

It was a place where the awakened gods could speak to each other. The space where he had been alone for so long was packed with the other gods for a short while, but now most of them had vanished. They had died, and in a way that made it difficult for them to come back to life in human form.

Sigh...

But then again, perhaps this was for the best.

"Greetings."

The gods that remained welcomed him back. They were the ones who had stayed alive by entrusting their holy object forms to other humans. The God of the Sun sighed as he saw they were less than twenty in number, but quickly smoothed out his face to look authoritative.

"Is she still unable to speak?" He gestured to the Goddess of Fire.

"Not yet." The God of the Moon shook his head. "But she's recovered quite a bit." They didn't have to speak formally because they were both great gods.

"That's a relief."

"Yes, it is. In more ways than one."

With the sleeping goddess nearby, the two gods sat facing each other.

"Time is still flowing normally."

The God of the Sun nodded at his calm statement. That was fortunate, despite everything else. Because this world was the real one, time flowed as it always had even though the God of Time, the devil, had died.

"It's fortunate indeed. He was born after time began to flow, not before it."

"But the child didn't know this. How fearless of her."

Scarlett Arman. Wouldn't she have thought that time might stop in her world?

The God of the Sun had nagged Baba for some time because of that. He had yelled at him for her recklessness, but this was something that even he couldn't deny.

"I have mixed feelings about the way things turned out, but perhaps this was the best result."

He had been on the fence about sacrificing the child in the first place.

The God of the Moon nodded. He could say this because they were the ones who survived. But the gods who had died were the ones who had never taken any action in anything.

Either way, this wasn't a bad ending.

In the silent space, the two gods quietly made a toast.

Meanwhile, Emperor Charlemagne Kalior asked Lady Scarlett Arman for her hand in marriage.

CHAPTER
ONE HUNDRED AND FORTY-SIX

The Fairies' Shelter. It was only natural that the Safe Zone around the Imperial Palace would be named thus.

"Tell the truth."

At the special place called the Shelter for short, Charlemagne spoke directly to the fairies. "You are now past the age to eat the fruit that Lett has kissed, aren't you?"

"Nuh-uh!"

"We're still young! Still babies!"

"Babies?" He wondered if they had killed their consciences the way they had killed the devil.

As he narrowed his eyes in a glare, the apple-loving Bell muttered with a pout, "Just... big babies!"

At the sight of the fairies mulishly arguing that they were going to be Scarlett's babies forever, Charlemagne gritted his teeth. His instinct was telling him that the creatures in front of him were not only as strong as he was, but their mental age was much greater than they were letting on.

"I, too, am a baby brother."

"You are twenty, from what I know."

"I was born again. So, I am only a year old."

Charlemagne gazed vacantly into the distance and sighed. "Fine."

"Fine?"

He didn't feel like dragging this on. The fairies' devious nature wasn't the reason he was here today.

"Cooperate with me, if that is the case."

He was here to exploit the creatures that wanted to remain Scarlett's "cute babies."

"Cooperate?" Glenn asked questioningly.

Charlemagne twisted one corner of his mouth into a smirk. "This will make Scarlett very happy."

"Me! I wanna do it!"

"I miss Lettie. Let's do it after we see her!"

"Yep, yep!"

Only Glenn, who had once been a twenty-year-old nobleman, looked unsettled. But since the three older fairies, who were like his brothers, had agreed, there was nothing he could do.

Sometime later, Charlemagne was standing in front of Scarlett in the Shelter.

"Scarlett."

Fireworks made of flowers were blooming all over the

Shelter. The faintly glowing petals in the night sky unfurled softly with the help of the fairies' lovely mana, which sparkled luminously. It was as if the stars had come down.

"If you could be happy with me…"

Charlemagne couldn't say that he would make her happy. He wasn't someone who was good enough to say that. Even if he had cleared up many of the false rumors, he was still going to be called a tyrant for the rest of his life. And though he was changing a little at a time, there was no way he could become the perfect sage king, because in the end, he still had usurped the throne. He knew that being his partner for eternity would be the furthest thing from happiness.

"If you could allow me that…"

But still… if she could accept him…

The man who had been covered in blood his whole life had found someone to love for the first time. In the beginning, he had simply enjoyed the feeling, but as time passed, he couldn't express the entirety of his emotions, which led him to say the word "happy" for the first time in his life.

"Will you marry me?"

The moon, which had gradually begun to shine over the world, softly brightened the area where the pair stood. Her golden hair captured a brilliance that no other light could follow. He missed her even as he gazed into her eyes. It was endearing.

She had been speechless ever since the fireworks had gone off, but her expression was changing every second. She blinked her eyes hard as if she was holding herself back, and the lips that she had clamped shut twitched anxiously many times.

Finally, she smiled.

It was a pleased smile—no, it was a *happy* smile. Charlemagne, who had been stiff and tense, finally relaxed, and so did his lips. Even before she could voice her response, he had a premonition.

Ah, I truly believe...

"Yes!"

...that I could become happy.

"So, I see that wedding dresses are white in this world, too."

"I am sorry, did you say something?"

"No, nothing."

Charlemagne asked me to marry him. I still remember that moment as if it was yesterday.

"I wanted to ask him first."

The maidservants helping me dress glanced at each other as they registered the words that had slipped from my mouth without meaning to. Lucy, who still regarded me as an incorrigible rascal even though I was now the mistress of the house, narrowed her eyes.

"You wanted to ask who what?"

"I wanted to ask His Majesty to marry me first."

Nancy's busy hands stopped moving as her eyes widened. After a brief silence, the maidservants burst into laughter.

"My goodness."

Even Lucy, who was becoming more like a resident assistant, snickered helplessly, her face red. "That is so like you, my lady... I mean, mistress."

"It is indeed!"

Today was the day of my wedding, and only a month since the proposal. I was wearing a snow-white wedding dress made of a material so soft it felt like it would melt, and my hair was done up elegantly. Several maidservants had to help with my dress because it was so delicate.

I can't tell if they're styling me or styling the dress. I felt like a mannequin that was being used to hold up the dress so it wouldn't wrinkle. Also, the wedding dress was ridiculously expensive.

"Are these pearls?"

"Of course not! They are diamonds. See how they sparkle?"

How are they so small and colorful, then? And is it even okay to use so many on a single dress?

Diamonds that were mixed with pink and blue swirled around the dress like stars. And not only that, but the same diamonds were on my necklace and on the tiara that was used to fix my veil as well.

What the actual f—

"There is powdered pearl in your dress as well. If I may say so, a mountain-high pile of powdered pearl was used to make the material for this dress."

I was speechless.

The diamonds weren't the only jewels; in fact, they were among the least impressive gemstones. However, I already knew about the other stones.

"Mistress, it is the first time I have ever seen fairy stones in person."

"Me too, mistress! They are so magical."

"Yes, they really are!"

I gave up on thinking any further and just nodded.

Yeah, I guess this is how weddings are. Something you could pour a waterfall of money into and not get slammed for—with a dress that would be worn only once and kept in the closet for the rest of my life or resold later.

"I can't let something like this shock me." Deciding to

stop being so surprised, I turned my eyes proudly toward the chest that held the tiara. No one had peeked at the tiara yet, so we all gazed at the chest, our eyes filled with both anticipation and fear.

Lucy's voice broke the thick silence. "We should hurry."

Which meant, "Hurry up and finish with the dress so we can look at the tiara."

The maidservants understood right away and moved their hands twice as fast as before. The feeling that I had become a mannequin settled twice as heavily as well, and I laughed hollowly.

Is this how the bride normally feels on her wedding day?

Was it because I was in a different world? I thought there would be more fondness or affection. I momentarily imagined Isar and the duchess coming to see me with tears in their eyes, but I shooed away that thought.

Ugh!

I also mentally waved away images of the elders with tears in their eyes. The truth was, everyone was displeased that my wedding was being held so soon. However, since I wasn't going to live somewhere else, they just congratulated me instead.

Tears look good on my fairy babies, but even Glenn crying is kind of...

And the advisors—they already cried yesterday. Of course, it wasn't because they felt any happiness or fondness about our wedding; They teared up because they were grateful I was marrying their wretched emperor.

That Commander of the Knights, too! Even Opere had kept humming like crazy, though I couldn't hear its words.

I let out a chuckle as I thought about everyone. This was totally different from all the wedding scenes I had remembered in movies.

"I didn't know things would turn out this way."

"What would, mistress?"

I had done everything I could to get dumped by the tyrant. It had been so hard for me, since I was such a normal, regular girl...

But anyway...

"Nothing. I was just thinking about my future family plans."

"F-family plans?"

Lucy's expression turned odd, but I didn't notice because I was thinking about how weird my life had been. I had been so certain that my future husband would never be the silver-haired tyrant.

"You never know what will happen in the future, you know?"

"Yes... but why are you already making family plans?"

"Hmm?" *What is she talking about?* "I've had plans ever since I met His Majesty."

But those plans had failed—failed very nicely.

Nah, this is a success!

I grinned like an idiot as I giggled, and Lucy's eyes shook violently.

"Right."

"What? What were you thinking about?"

"Nothing, mistress. Please live a happy life."

"You're changing the subject! So cruel!"

"All right, all done! Now for the last piece!" Lucy cunningly ended the conversation and pointed to the chest with the tiara. The maidservants, whose shoulders had been shaking quietly for some reason, got to their feet, and carefully brought over the chest.

When they opened it, even I couldn't stop my mouth from falling open.

The fairy stone that Glenn had given me to use on this tiara was amazing, but I never imagined...

The multicolored fairy stone was so brilliant that even diamonds could never compare. The white tiara, designed so that the fairy stone wouldn't stand out too much on its own, had a slight glow of pink to it—yet was very soft, so it wouldn't be too stark. There were also roses carved into the tiara, and upon looking down, I saw that my dress had a similar rose motif.

"It is beautiful," someone commented, and we all nodded.

The tiara was slowly lowered onto my head with reverence, and the veil was laid down with a soft *swish*. Finally, after being dressed in the pinnacle of luxury that I thought I'd never be able to move in, I carefully made my way to the wedding hall.

Isar, who was surprisingly crying and blowing his nose, escorted me as he held my hand. He grumbled about why I was getting married so soon and refused to give my hand over to Charlemagne, but Charlemagne coolly made him let go. Isar hmphed like a pouting child and whirled around to find his seat.

Ridiculous. I stopped myself from laughing as I watched his antics, but that didn't last long. My eyes were drawn to Charlemagne like a magnet.

Just look at those lips. He looks even more beautiful than I do. No, more beautiful than anyone else in this world.

His lips look so sweet.

"And the bride..."

And he's totally mine now!

I answered, "I do," a few times to the officiator.

"You may now ki—Oh my!"

The moment Charlemagne lifted my veil, I jumped onto my tiptoes and engulfed his lips with mine. As my lips curled upward in satisfaction at the soft feeling, he held the back of my head and my waist as he slowly...

"Ugh! Seriously? I did not think I would see such a blatant display at a wedding!"

"Bwahahaha!"

...and deeply...

"Umm..."

...kissed me.

When I gazed into his face a long while later, I saw that he looked incredibly happy. His eyes were dark with a deep satisfaction as well as passionate desire.

"Is the wedding over now?"

"Y-yes, Your Majesty."

He swept me up into his arms and flew to the palace so quickly that my dress barely touched the ground. And then, we...

...we had our happy ending.

The important thing was how fortunate it was that I had failed to get dumped by the tyrant.

Just as I was about to praise my failed plans, I suddenly

remembered. *My bouquet landed on the chancellor's head, didn't it? This world has a superstition about that too!*

Then, the chancellor will get married in three months?

"Being single forever isn't so bad, Chancellor. Charlemagne will gladly gift you a cat."

"Damn it! Damn it all! This is a nightmare!"

Well, there was one unhappy person, but whatever.

May our future be filled with only happiness, forever and ever.

The End.

CHAPTER ONE

On a beautiful clear day, fairy Glenn was floating around, deep in thought.

"Whatcha doin?"

"Are you crying, little brother? Are you ticklish? You asleep?"

Glenn shook his head, watching his older brother fairies giggle as they shot random questions at him, and then sighed. Now, they looked to be about thirteen years of age, and he suddenly realized how quickly time had passed.

"What's the matter?" Nell tilted his head as he asked Glenn. Nell was the fairy he thought the most capable of having a normal conversation.

Glenn's lower lip protruded as he answered, looking serious, "I need to choose a gift."

"A gift for Lettie?" Nell understood immediately. Everyone pondered the same question around this time of year. The other two fairies glanced over at him and Nell as they laughed and chattered away.

"I don't have anything to give her," Glenn said sullenly.

Big sister Scarlett was the empress and the lord of the House of Arman, and there was practically nothing in this world that she couldn't have.

"I want to give her something too. Let's think about it together."

Glenn nodded at Nell's words.

"Let's give her a watch!" the red-haired Bell shouted, joining in the conversation. He was highly interested in new inventions these days and wanted a magic watch. "Or a music box! Or apple jam! There's also a machine that makes jam!" Bell became more and more excited as he talked about the things he wanted. He chortled with delight as he frantically zoomed around in the air.

Glenn watched him coldly. "She probably already has all of that," he muttered.

Nell's eyes sparkled. "Then, let's give her something only we fairies can make!"

"Something only we can make?" Glenn's eyes began to shine as well.

"Yeah! Fairy stones!"

"We already give her those," Glenn said.

Nell looked disheartened.

"No, no!" Gill, who was watching them, cried out, his blue hair quivering. "We make other things, too!"

The other three fairies turned their eyes to him in confusion.

"We can make babies!" Gill said triumphantly.

"Babies!"

Nell and Bell looked like they'd had a sudden realization, but Glenn tilted his head in confusion, a strange expression on his face.

"Babies?"

"Right, you don't know this. Babies grow on trees."

"What?"

"Nuh-uh!" Nell blurted out before Glenn could ask further, shaking his head vigorously. "Human babies are brought by birds!"

"Huh? Then, what are the fruits?"

"Probably the same as us fairies! We were born from flowers," Nell explained coaxingly, acting all grown up.

"Uhh, guys?"

"Then, what kind of bird brings human babies?"

Glenn's eyes shook fiercely as he watched his brothers. He knew what Nell was going to say.

"A bird from the Alang Tree gets a baby from the sky and gives it to the humans."

No... Glenn didn't know where to begin, but he had a feeling he knew why his fairy brothers were saying all these things.

I know they've begun developing quite an interest in the human world, but...

The problem was that they were only remembering what they wanted to see. Because of that, the only thing they knew about babies was what they had read in fairy tales. And of course, children's storybooks would depict having a baby being brought to a family by a bird.

"Are you planning on becoming a bird, then?" Glenn asked sulkily, unable to bring himself to explain exactly how babies were made. "I don't know how to transform yet," he remarked. He was about to suggest coming up with a different gift.

Nell spoke patronizingly once more. "You don't have to transform because you're still a baby."

An ominous feeling washed over Glenn. "What does that mean? Explain your idea in detail."

"A baby's a baby, so just be a baby."

"Yeah, yeah! That's right!"

Even Bell nodded in agreement.

Glenn stared at his brothers in horror. He realized why he was so terrified when Gill hollered excitedly, "We can be the birds!"

"What are you... Ugh."

The three older fairies were always treating Glenn like

a baby based on the difference in their powers. They waved their chubby hands through the air, and Glenn's eyes slowly began to close.

"Aww, look! Our baby brother won't be a baby for long."

"Yeah, he is falling asleep at once!"

"Good boy! So good! I'm so proud!"

I'm glad their vocabulary has increased, but I really wish they wouldn't say they were proud of something like this.

And with that final thought, Glenn fell into a deep sleep.

As he lay in the flowerbed, his breath evening out peacefully, the three older fairies stood around him exchanging looks. They had all been racking their brains for what to gift Lettie for her birthday, and it was good that they had come up with this idea.

"But Lettie said it's too soon for a baby."

"A baby's too soon? What does that mean?"

"Maybe she means it's too soon to meet a baby because they take a long time to come," Nell butted in. Gill and Bell gazed admiringly at him, and he grinned shyly before shouting, "It's nice we had a baby close by!"

"Yeah! Our baby brother's the best!"

"That's right!"

The three fairies began gathering bunches of flowers, but they didn't just pluck them; they dug them up by the roots and even planted some around Glenn. It was a catastrophe brought on by the fairies' lack of understanding of what a "gift" was.

Meanwhile, Glenn enjoyed the sweet, albeit forced, nap he hadn't had in a long time, blissfully unaware that doodles of flowers were being drawn on his face.

For some reason, the little grins on the three fairies surrounding the sleeping Glenn looked evil.

Lady Peridot Fletta was in the midst of training to control the power that had been bestowed upon her during the dark wizards' invasion. She didn't want to break someone's hand during a handshake ever again.

Never. Again.

Craaash!

The man who had fought alongside her—and had his hand crushed—Chancellor Clover, remained silent as he stared at the area where a small shack had been blasted away by a punch from the lady. He looked up at the sky and sighed.

Rubbing his forehead, he cautiously stepped to the side. Then he turned to Lady Fletta, looking pale. "Uhh, well, His Majesty did say he would knight those who received powers during the incident, but there is no need to push yourself, Lady Fletta."

"I didn't push myself," Lady Fletta retorted bitterly. "I really didn't, but I'm scared I might crush someone's head next, not just their hand... Chancellor?"

"Ahem... It's n-nothing." The more he saw the lady, the more aggressive she seemed to be.

The way she talks, and that power she has!

How could she say that in front of the man whose hand she had nearly crushed to powder? Was she threatening him because he saw how she couldn't control her power?

Is she telling me she'll smash my head next? Damn it.

The chancellor inwardly cursed the Minister of Information, who was supposed to have been here originally. "Wh-what I mean is that you do not need to feel rushed."

"But I'm not even allowed to leave this place until I can control my power. What if I never get to leave?"

"Ah, that is an unnecessary concern. You have, ahem, g-gotten better since the first day of training."

"Have I really?"

The pair silently stared at the place where the shack had been for a moment.

"The remnants have shattered in a far tidier manner, haven't they?"

"Is that... a good thing?"

"Yes, of course, Lady Fletta." Sycophantic flattery dripped from his voice, belying his nickname of the Iron Chancellor. "So, please do not be hasty. Focus just a tad more, and I believe you will get there soon."

And stop calling over busy people to check on your progress!

Several people had been chosen by the holy objects and developed unique abilities. His Majesty, the Emperor had ordered that they all learned how to manage their powers above all priorities, but...

She can't call me over here every two days!

The chancellor was troubled because he was now practically in charge of Lady Peridot Fletta's training.

Just because we fought side by side. The elders of Arman were there, too!

"Well then, I shall take my leave now, Lady Fletta."

"All right. Safe travels, Chancellor."

The weapon of mass destruction, who was also the lady of superhuman strength, said her goodbyes and turned back around to continue her training.

Craaash!

Hastily putting the deafening racket behind him, the chancellor bolted to his office. On his way, he was teased about the bags under his eyes reaching his knees by Empress

Scarlett, who was just passing by.

"Damn! Damn it all!"

It had been almost three months since the wedding—no—since the time he had caught the bouquet.

SIDE STORY
CHAPTER TWO

"Hey, the chancellor says he's too exhausted from dealing with Lady Fletta. What do you think about that?" I asked Isar in passing.

"That's not my problem," he replied indifferently.

"Poor guy." I gave a little groan and turned around to look at the chancellor, whose lower jaw was trembling.

"So, he says."

"Th-that's... that's just harsh!" the chancellor cried out, fuming in a way he never usually did. "To be honest, the people of the House of Arman were closer in proximity to the lady than I was during that time!"

It was true. Isar and the elders were the ones who had fought by her side when the holy objects had flown to them. They said that the chancellor only joined them afterwards. Isar had scuttled far away from Lady Fletta when he saw her massive strength, and the chancellor had stepped into his place shortly after his arrival.

Too bad he ended up with them in the first place.

The chancellor said that he had left the temple to see how things were going outside, thinking that a battle between the gods wasn't something he should get involved in. Unfortunately for him, he headed in the direction of Isar's group and ended up being stuck with them.

"Still, it's better than my brother going."

"That does not comfort me in the slightest."

"It wasn't meant to."

The chancellor scowled. I was sure he was swearing to himself again.

After staring at the chancellor for a moment, I glanced at Isar. His eyes were glued to the documents in his hands. The way he was passionately dealing with the paperwork was...

"Kind of sad, isn't it?"

"My situation is much worse."

"No, wait, mine is! I have empress work on top of my work as the lord of the House of Arman. And the duchess won't leave me alone, either."

The truth was that it wasn't *that* bad, thanks to the power of the Goddess of Fire that had been helping me. But I was still exhausted.

"I know everything I do and learn will eventually come in handy, but trying to memorize the history of our house in addition to all the work I have to do is killing me. And that's not all! Why do I have to worry about so many things when I have tea? Just browsing through the list of noble and foreign manners and etiquette wears me down to the bone," I murmured slowly.

Then, I whipped my head around to look at the chancellor. He flinched at my drained gaze.

"I'm sorry, what were you saying earlier? Something about wanting to be removed from overseeing Lady Fletta's training, right?"

The chancellor avoided my eyes. I thought of my husband's facial expressions and attempted a cold smile. The chancellor glanced shiftily at me, and his eyes became round when he saw my expression.

"Chancellor, I would have gone to Lady Fletta myself if she hadn't told me she was the most comfortable with you. Did you know that?"

Are you kidding me?

I had to jump right into mountains of work the moment I returned from my honeymoon. I hadn't even been able to play with my fairy kings because I was overwhelmed by the workload! The House of Arman was in shambles—more than anyone could ever imagine—because the previous lord hadn't done any bit of proper work. No matter how many exceptional aides and elders there were, they couldn't touch the work that was meant for the lord. I seriously wanted to murder that stupid man when I found out.

I wondered if it would be beneficial to find Baba and bring him back from his carefree journey around the world to help me out. I didn't know if he was any good at paperwork, but I thought he would do an okay job if someone made him do it. Also, I was annoyed that he was the only one who had time to relax.

Deciding to send a search party to find him later, I turned back to the chancellor. "Well, I suppose if you're that frightened of the lady, we could switch jobs—"

"No, Your Majesty!" the chancellor shouted.

"That's nonsense!" Isar bellowed at the same time.

Nice reactions! Wait, Isar?

Apparently, he was listening to everything we were saying, even as he pretended to be so immersed in his work.

"Hmph, why not? I'm friends with the lady, so I'm sure she'll be comfortable enough with me."

"She said herself that she was 'most comfortable' with me, though!"

"Do you know how hard it was to make her keep her distance from the House of Arm—" Isar covered his mouth with his hand to keep himself from revealing more.

The chancellor and I glared at him with narrowed eyes.

"What did you do?"

"You did something?"

"I, uh... I have a lot of work to do..."

These people!

I clicked my tongue at the two grown men who were afraid of the lady's power. "Whatever the case, enough with the grouching. Chancellor, you'll continue to take care of the lady. Lady Pere... Plea... Wait, I mean..."

"Lady Peridot Fletta."

"Yes, Peridot Fletta. It might do you good to get close to Lady Fletta," I mumbled sullenly, thinking about how hard it was to remember her name. The chancellor, who had piped up to correct me, scowled at my response.

You don't dislike her. I knew it the moment you said her full name.

I lazily waved my hand and told him to leave.

"Go ask her out on a date or something. Of course, it would have to be inside the Arman estate. The lady loves compliments, so complimenting her often will work. Anyway, you may leave. I need to hurry up and finish this so I can go see my husband."

I haven't seen my fairy kings lately, either. I had heard Glenn call the three innocent little fairies "big brother," but I hadn't been able to ask when he had started calling them that.

"D-date?" the chancellor stammered, blanching. He

then rolled his eyes as he left the room.

As the door to the office closed, Isar said indifferently, "The duchess will get on my case if that man gets married."

"About what? Getting married?"

"Yeah."

I was surprised that he didn't seem as offended by this as he used to be, even though he still looked displeased. The duchess, who had acquired the powers of soundproofing, had become softer than before, though I didn't know if that was because of her powers. But I did notice she had recently started working with the elders to talk to Isar about marriage.

In my eyes, she just liked having excuses to talk to him more. After all, Isar got irritated with her but at least didn't despise her enough to go for her throat. But I supposed things might be different in his shoes.

"Don't worry. I'll make sure you live your entire life as a male spinster." I beamed, and Isar gave me an unsettled look.

"Do you really have to go that far?"

"I said don't worry! Hmm, let's see... There are many ways, you know?"

I could publicly announce that he's devoted himself solely to a god, for instance. Or make him perfect in every way except in one important part of his body. Or make him more popular with the young lords rather than the ladies, so...

"Whatever you're thinking, stop."

"I didn't say anything! Why are you grinding your teeth?"

"You just twitched at my words!" he said.

"Because I was startled when you suddenly started talking!"

"You, the lord of the house? Startled? Don't make me laugh. Do you feel bad for the people that you 'startle' like five times a day?"

"No, I don't! And stop exaggerating. I'm not scaring them. I'm making them laugh!"

"It's both, dummy!"

"What does that matter anyway?"

"You said you were startled!"

"So? Am I not allowed to be surprised? Oh, my husband! Big brother Isar is nagging at me." I exaggeratedly pretended to bawl and call for Charlemagne.

Isar looked horrified and clamped a hand across my mouth. "Are you insane? Why would you actually call—"

"Lett, did you call me?" Charlemagne glared at Isar's hand, which was covering my mouth.

My eyes curved into a smile at the man who had appeared in front of me within a few seconds. The teleportation bracelet that Baba had given us as a wedding present was put to work several times a day, whether we were busy or not.

We are in our honeymoon phase, you know.

With a gasp, Isar let go and jumped away from me, looking terrified.

"You're always so quick-footed," Charlemagne muttered, implying that he would have chopped off that hand if he had been a moment too slow in removing it.

Isar wiped the cold sweat from his face and sighed. "Welcome, Your Majesty... again."

At first, the people of the estate had turned pale and bowed whenever Charlemagne appeared in the mansion, but now they were more comfortable with seeing him around. That was good for everyone.

Charlemagne watched Isar for a moment with narrowed eyes and then, without replying, turned his head to look at me. The way the warmth immediately crossed over his face was so endearing that I just had to stand up and kiss him on the lips.

One kiss was all it took.

"Ugh!" Isar hastily gathered up the papers he was working on and dashed out of the room.

"You arrived just when I was starting to miss you."

"You called for me just when *I* was starting to miss *you*."

The lights in the office dimmed as we whispered to each other.

Inwardly applauding Isar for not forgetting his work even when he was appalled, I sat on the empty desk, which Opere had heated up, to spend time with Charlemagne.

Opere, who had resisted at first, grouchily telling Charlemagne not to use him in this manner...

The Goddess of Fire, who had been waking up enough to talk to me again...

And the God of the Moon, who had begun speaking to Charlemagne little by little...

"Let's give Lettie her present early!"

"Yeah, or else we'll forget!"

"Our little brother will cry if we make him sleep until her birthday! Let's... Wh-what, huh?"

And the fairy kings, who had transformed into birds and were floating outside the office window, holding the sleeping baby Glenn...

...all turned their heads, went back to sleep, or scurried away from us.

SIDE STORY
CHAPTER THREE

Peridot Fletta was in the middle of a meal when she heard a whisper.

– You are a god…

It was a whisper like that of a snake. Of course, she pretended she didn't hear anything.

– You can become a god!

She had begun hearing this ominous whispering a few days ago, when she was sniffling in her room because she couldn't control her newfound power.

– Are you sad? Are you tormented?

Sniff. "Hmm?"

– I shall obliterate all that made you feel that way. I shall kill them all. Anything is possible with the power of a great god. I shall lend you my power!

Even the children playing heroes and demon lords out in the streets wouldn't say something this asinine.

Still, the hissing whispers brought her to her senses. Peridot Fletta wiped away her tears, got to her feet, and demolished her bed.

"There must be a fly buzzing around somewhere," she

muttered to herself.

At her menacing tone, the voice paused, but a moment later, it began whispering again, in a lightly trembling voice.

– Ch-child, who possesses the power of a god...

Crack!

A dresser went flying across the room.

– You are m-my successor...

Boom! Crash!

"Why are there so many flies these days? I should go and punch down some trees or someth—"

– Enough... Enough! The voice shouted hastily and let out a scream, just as she was about to jump out of her window and down into the yard. *Damn it! Why did I have to be paired with someone like this?!*

Hmm...

Peridot thought the voice had been gone ever since then, but judging by the hissing she was hearing in her ear right now, it hadn't vanished after all.

– Don't you want to become a god?

Ignore it. Just ignore it.

The voice was incredibly creepy, and it would have terrified someone more fainthearted. However, Peridot had fought demons before, even if it was just that one time. Not to mention that her first impression of this voice was already bad.

I should still report it though, right?

Pretending she couldn't hear the voice until the end of her meal, Peridot stood up.

I could hear that voice not once, but twice. I think it's because of that holy object the empress told me about.

She wasn't the only one who had been chosen by a god and given powers during the battle with the demons that appeared in the capital, but she had never heard of anyone else experiencing the same thing she was. The voice itself wasn't scary, but hearing it was foreboding. She decided to hurry.

– Hey. Hey! What are you doing, child?!

"Since when did flies learn how to speak?"

In the end, Peridot decided to just send a letter to Chancellor Clover's personal home.

Well, he is my supervisor. If he can't fix it, I'll probably have to go to Her Majesty. Or maybe even the emperor himself!

That was what truly terrified her. She nervously chewed on her nail.

– Can't you hear me? How dare you ignore me like this?

"Shut up. I'm trying to figure out how to get rid of you. So, stay quiet."

– What?!

Did it understand me?

With that strangled gasp, the voice didn't speak again.

I hope this is the end of it.

Even though she'd only heard it twice, she could tell that the owner of the voice was a coward. It was probably just scared.

Before even an hour had passed, the chancellor arrived.

Huff, huff! "Lady Fletta!" He looked completely lucid and urgent, which was rare.

Peridot let out a sigh. *Why do I get the feeling that this man won't have any answers?*

The thought that she may have to see His and Her Majesties crossed her mind.

"Hmph," I scoffed, lying in Charlemagne's arms on the couch in his office.

"What's wrong?"

"It's this." I waved a letter, and Charlemagne gazed at it with cold eyes.

"What's Baba saying this time?"

A blue bird had appeared over our heads while we were enjoying a lazy afternoon after an intimate exchange. When I opened my eyes, the bird handed me the fluttering letter and disappeared. It was from Baba.

"I couldn't find him no matter how hard I searched, and here he is, just telling me where he is."

"Hmm. Let me see." Charlemagne's face hardened as his eyes traveled down the page. Rightfully so, since the content wasn't good news.

"The East Continent..."

"It seems he's been secretly hiding around over there. That's why the spies couldn't find him."

I inwardly cursed our friend as I recalled how he had dropped in for a moment before leaving with the wind again.

What did he give us for our wedding present again? Oh right, he gave us laxatives.

He said that it was to lessen the wrath of the gods that survived, but I honestly felt like it was more of a prank.

Thankfully, we hadn't taken any, but the chancellor had drunk the wine with the laxatives. The bags under his eyes from that incident still hadn't shrunk.

Tsk! Anyway...

The issue wasn't our cheeky friend, who had tossed us laxatives at the wedding and disappeared. The issue was the content of the letter he had sent.

"To think that holy objects flew to that part of the continent as well..."

Those who had fought in the capital weren't the only

ones who'd received them. According to Baba, most of them had remained in the capital, but a few had flown far, far away. Three objects had transferred from person to person, unable to find a suitable vessel, and ended up on the East Continent.

"He's taken care of two of them, so we should forgive him for the prank he pulled at the wedding."

Charlemagne kissed my forehead with a chuckle. "If you say so, my love."

We laughed good-naturedly, and our lips entwined for a moment before we returned to the subject we were discussing.

"He says he'll take care of the remaining object, so that's good, but…"

"The problem is that there's an object near us that has other plans."

Charlemagne pressed his lips against my forehead again.

"Seriously?" I couldn't stop the corners of my lips from creeping upward even as I tried to be serious.

Charlemagne stared at me as I sat up and turned to face him. His slightly curved eyes twinkled playfully. There had been a time when I could never have imagined seeing this side of him.

Taking a firm grasp of my thoughts, which were about to become entranced by him, I pretended to be serious. "This is important. We are discussing matters of state, Your Majesty."

"Didn't you promise not to call me that?"

Charlemagne let out a low laugh as I coughed at his teasing words. We had agreed to call each other whatever was shortest after the wedding.

"Charl," I corrected myself and then tapped the letter. "Perhaps it's a good thing that none of the other gods are great gods, minus a few."

Most of the gods we had done away with while we got rid of the devil were great gods, so the only ones left were Baba's God of the Sun, my Goddess of Fire, and Charlemagne's God of the Moon.

"He said the other gods were middle or low tier."

I thought about the God of the Moon and the Goddess of Fire, who were probably lounging in their subspace dimension, teasing the God of the Sun.

"So, it might not be too troublesome no matter what any god does…"

"But a god's still a god, so it'll be troublesome if someone gets caught up in their exploits." Charlemagne regarded the letter coldly as he replied to my concerns.

"You're right."

"We haven't received reports about any strange reactions in the capital."

"According to this letter, the vessel won't be able to control their power, or may have a breakdown and go berserk, or..."

The door of the office burst open. Charlemagne turned his head and saw the chancellor barge in, looking harried. I continued reading, my eyes following a vague human shadow behind him right outside the door.

"Or hear v—"

"Lady Fletta is hearing voices!"

"—voices. What?"

"She says a fly keeps buzzing in her ear! That's why she destroyed her bed... and no, I'm scared!"

"Greetings, Your Majesty, and Your Majesty as well." At the chancellor's cry of horror, Lady Peridot Fletta hastily entered the room and greeted us. Cold sweat beaded on her forehead. She looked at the chancellor with a baffled look on her face. "I am the one hearing voices, so I do not know why the chancellor is saying he is scared."

Yeah, I agree. Destroying a wooden bed isn't that... Well, no, it's pretty scary.

After all, it was a bed in a nobleman's house, which meant that it was probably secured to the floor and magically reinforced for sturdiness.

Okay, that's terrifying. This surpasses a superhuman level of strength.

The chancellor's cheeks trembled as he stared at the lady in disbelief, but he couldn't make any retorts. I watched, feeling kind of bad for him.

"Please come in."

While Scarlett greeted Lady Fletta to learn what was going on in detail, Charlemagne began to pen a reply to Baba's letter. He decided not to speak to Lady Fletta himself because people tended to freeze in fear when he did so.

"Well then, hmm, Charl? Could you write and ask about how to overpower a holy object, please?"

"Sure."

In another part of the world, Baba was traveling to recover the remaining rogue holy object. A blue bird landed on his shoulder while he was in the midst of searching.

"Ah, they're so quick with getting work done," he murmured. But he wasn't pleased for long. The moment he unfolded the letter, he had to stuff it back into his pockets again without being able to read it. "This continent is chaotic as well."

It had become even more so when the Pan's Assassins were obliterated by Charlemagne. *Who would have thought that the organization was the main force behind the political power in these lands?*

Anyway, the chaos that had started after the annihilation of that force brought even more disorder to the smaller nations, and the holy objects had taken advantage of that opportunity to find vessels here. And...

"There it is."

The god of the holy object, who had different plans, was coming toward him.

Or rather, the owner of the holy object was coming toward him.

Just once more. If I could see them just once more...

They were nothing but recollections now. Recollections of everything she had lost.

Even the dandelions that grew on the stone wall in front of the school gates had shone brightly back then. But she couldn't see any of that now as she stared at the moonlight that filtered through the white window.

They had all given their lives, one by one, for that sickly prince. She couldn't understand them at all. What kind of hope had they seen in the last royal of a ruined country? They all had brilliant futures; no one could deny that. Not like her, who had everything and was yet so faded. They had nothing, but they were dazzling.

She had loved them.

But then... they had all died, and the only one left now was the small prince.

"Yes. Just him."

The young prince didn't cry. He only stared up at her, his lips stiff with an inscrutable expression.

Yes, they had asked her to protect him. It was the dying wish of her last friend.

"Come."

He was such a small child, so it would be better if she ran with him in her arms. She knew that in her head, but she didn't want to do it. She was barely pushing down the urge to kill him and blame him for everything.

"Don't touch me if you know what's good for you."

The child winced at her cold words. Uncaring, she began moving at a fast pace that was difficult for a child to follow and could hear him struggling to catch up behind her. She did not have time to waste, but she did not want to pick him up.

No, she couldn't.

If I kill you now, they'll be sad.

That one thought was holding her back from killing him. Sorrow washed over her. "I miss them," she murmured, almost to herself, as she stood in place, waiting for the child to catch up. The path she was taking to escape was full of her memories with them, even though it would be faster to find one that wasn't.

The second the boy came close enough, she firmly grabbed the back of his collar, being careful to touch as little of his skin as possible. She began running at top speed.

It was close.

She arrived at the entrance of her destination within five minutes and then turned around. The boy looked up at her with trembling eyes. It seemed like he was about to cry, but he never let out a single tear.

She spoke involuntarily. "I never imagined that this would be my last moment. I would have been on the other side if it weren't for my friends' request." She would have cried out for vain revenge, on the side that thirsted for the child's death. "I don't know if you are worth saving. I don't know why..."

She was sad that the words "I don't know why they all died for you" couldn't pass her lips. She couldn't speak about their deaths, and it seemed the child would break down if he heard them too.

Her throat contracting painfully, she groaned, "I don't know why they loved you."

Yes, I don't understand. Why? Why did they? Why did they do so much for you?

Breathing hard, she grasped the boy's shoulder and pressed her forehead against his, trembling.

"You'd better survive," she said. "I'm leaving first, so you need to prove to me that you are worth all the sacrifice."

The pale, white face of the boy gradually hardened.

Yes, that's good enough, she thought. She was finally sure that he would survive.

"Don't forget that the cost of my life is very expensive," she said as she let go of the boy. Just then, arrows whistled through the air. She covered the boy with her body and flung open the door, roughly throwing him inside.

Ignoring the incomprehensible voice of the boy behind her, she turned back around.

Boom!

The door slammed shut the instant he was inside, as the space could only hold one person. He would have to stay in there for the next ten years or so. If he had the skills, he would be able to survive and come back out.

The child—no, the prince—was now safe.

"Damn! Are we too late?"

A man squatted down next to her as he cursed. His rat face looked familiar.

"Hi, Clyden!" She caught her ragged breath, trying to recover at least a bit of stamina as she waved. The vermin glared at her as he ground his teeth.

"It's been a while, hasn't it? How's that jaw I smashed last year?" she asked, as if asking how his parents were.

The man twitched and covered his jaw with his hand.

She laughed at his reaction, continuing with a grin. "I'm guessing the jaw is working fine, considering how you're gritting your teeth like that. What's been going on with you to make you look even scruffier than before?"

"You bitch. I'm surprised you can blab like that in this situation."

"Oh, wow. I didn't ask because I was curious, but you are quite passionate in your response. I've been meaning to ask: Are you fond of me or something?"

Grit.

She gave him a disdainful look, believing that his jaw might shatter again from the constant grinding of his teeth. More people had appeared around them as she continued speaking with Clyden. She grinned even more widely as she chatted away.

"All right. I've waited patiently enough, so I trust that you'll mind your manners."

"Bullshit!"

"Such foul language. You can't even talk properly without cursing, can you? Tsk, tsk," she said, chastising the rat-face man.

She loosely stretched her limbs and readied her blade when someone else shouted at her.

"My lady! Your house will not be harmed if you surrender now!"

"If it isn't the chairman. How wonderful to see you!" Genuinely pleased at seeing the chairman with his long, navy hair, she beamed as she greeted him. They had a good relationship before all this happened, and it was a relief that she could see him one last time before she died.

Hesitation briefly crossed his face before he hardened his voice again. "Please, I advise you to surrender!"

"House or whatever, forget them all. They don't mean anything. Let them eat dirt."

People from her "esteemed" house had killed her friends. She heard someone shouting curses at her, but she didn't reply.

Eventually, she lifted her blade. Her swordsmanship had improved suddenly of late, so she felt she could take about half of the people here down with her.

I must take at least half of them with me for my friends to welcome me. She briefly wondered if she should let the chairman live.

It was crazy, but she couldn't contain her laughter. It felt like they were right there with her. She gave a joyful smile.

And in that final moment...

"Why are you even here? What kind of empress has so much time on her hands?"

"Hmph. I had a feeling you'd hide instead of returning, you know?"

"Th-there's no way I would do that."

"Look me in the eyes when you say that."

"And I'm not the only one here, either."

...she saw them.

"Wh-what?"

"Charl, and the poor chancellor, who was the victim of your prank, are here. Lady Peridot Fletta is here too."

"Who's that?"

"Lady Peridot Fletta? Oh... She's the owner of *that* holy object we assume we have on our side."

Craaash!

"Is this good enough?"

"Amazing."

"Please, please make someone else supervise her, Your Majesty."

"I think you'll do a great job."

"Excuse me."

She stared at the wall that had appeared suddenly, separating her from where the prince was hidden. It had been created by a lady, using her fist, even though she had never held a blade before in her life.

"You know what? Let me ask you now since we're on the subject... Why would you just tell me to 'take care of it'? You should tell me how!"

"Oh..."

"Oh? Don't be ridiculous!"

"But following me all the way here is..."

"What?"

"You really didn't want to work, did you?"

"Hehe."

"If you've got so much time on your hands, can you make your gods stop picking on my God of the Sun?"

"Psh! They won't listen to us. Just give up."

The playful banter between these strange new people clashed with the somber atmosphere around them.

SIDE STORY
CHAPTER FIVE

Aness Dunn was the bastard child of a duke from the Noahd kingdom in the East Continent. Her homeland, which was built upon one of the few fertile regions in the desert lands of the east, was beautiful. Noahd, the blessed kingdom that had four seasons, was also known as the land of tourism, trade, and gold.

It was said that the Fairy King of the Earth had fallen asleep there, which was why the lands were abnormally fertile even in the middle of the desert. Unfortunately, the country built on those blessed lands never had a peaceful day.

How it had grown to be the central pillar of the East Continent as its culture and civilization developed was now a story from long ago. The Academy remained pure, but it was merely the best of a bad bunch. Each tier of society was rotten to the core, and every gifted person felt that it was better to become a citizen of a different country and proceeded to leave as soon as they possibly could.

And in that fertile land that was rotting away, Aness Dunn was born as the bastard child of a duke.

"You must not draw attention to yourself and stay quiet."

That was what her mother had said even as she died.

Even when someone from the duke's house came for her, having recognized her natural talent.

Even when she returned home after following that person to the main house, unable to stand the cruel treatment by the heirs.

Even when she had entered the Academy with the support of the duke, whom she hated, because fighting with a sword was all she knew.

"Never let them see who you truly are."

Her mother had always been afraid they would snatch away her only living family.

But Aness had never feared the duke and his family. "They would never stand a chance against me," Aness muttered to herself. At the same time, she stared at the strange new people who appeared in front of her with impeccable timing.

The original people who were after her shouted and cursed on the other side of the wall that had just been created, but they scattered like leaves when they got a taste of that green-haired lady's powerful fist.

If I knew this would happen...

She probably wouldn't have locked the young king behind that door. Perhaps it would have been better to seek asylum in a different country with that fragile child instead of enduring an unexpected ten-year wait.

No... How can I trust these people?

Their timing was too perfect. They could be a different group of pursuers. But despite her wariness, she found herself telling this strange group everything about her past.

"Hmm? Oh, this is my power," someone told her before a sudden campfire appeared out of nowhere.

Her surprise at the sudden appearance of a campfire lasted for only a moment. Was it because the flames were so warm? Or was it because the scent of the soup in the pot placed on the fire was so heavenly?

If that isn't it, then...

The sounds of the soup bubbling.

The sounds of the fire crackling quietly.

The sounds of the peaceful chatter of voices.

The warmth and the deep affection seen in the eyes of these strangers—well, mainly that one couple over there— around her.

They don't seem to be after me, no matter how I look at them.

Her instincts, which had been honed for survival, were screaming at her. But in the end, these people had nothing to do with the current circumstances.

And they're immensely powerful.

Aness discreetly studied the people sitting around her. Putting aside the splendid outward appearance of that man, Charl, she felt he was the most powerful person in the group. She always measured a person by whether she could beat them, but she couldn't even fathom how strong he was.

Even my master didn't give off such an aura.

Also, the blade he was holding was unusual. The occasional humming noises it made gave her chills.

Is it an ego sword? No, it can't be. She'd only heard rumors about them. It couldn't be an ego sword. *Or can it?*

It could, and it probably was. But it didn't matter. His aura still raised the hairs on her arms, even though it wasn't sharp or exuding the intent to kill. He was simply smiling at his woman with the sweetest look in his eyes.

But still... he doesn't feel... human.

Aness looked away, feeling cautious about even the slightest glance toward the man. She then shifted her eyes to the woman who had treated her most kindly.

Was her name Lett? No, that was probably a nickname. Perhaps her name was Letia? Or Carlett?

Come to think of it, we haven't even exchanged our names because everything was so hectic. They had just built a wall and made a camp inside it, with Aness by their side.

Then again, what do names matter?

She got chills again as she watched the woman, Lett. She felt nonhuman as well, just like the man.

Is it true that couples become alike? Or maybe similar people just find each other.

What was clear was that any possibility of Aness leaving this place of her own volition had vanished because of those two.

Truly she didn't even have to study the other three, but she decided to humor herself. The main thing that she noticed about that man, Clover, were the bags under his eyes, rather than his handsome face. He would flinch whenever he glanced at the green-haired lady, who was apparently named Lady Peridot Fletta, but would still constantly talk to her whenever she seemed to be pushing herself or looked to need advice.

Is he scared of her? Does he find her difficult? Or are they romantically involved?

Aness was ignorant when it came to romantic relationships, but the relationship that these two shared made even her head tilt in confusion. Clover would scowl and take a step back from the lady, but then would take two steps closer when he spoke to her. Lady Fletta didn't care if he came close or retreated, but he would be the first person she looked for when something happened.

And as for their strengths... That man, Clover, didn't look too strong, but he didn't seem weak either. She had a strange feeling that her future generations would be cursed if she tried to harm him. It was common sense to stay far away from those kinds of people.

As for Lady Fletta... *She feels familiar for some reason.*

Aness didn't know about holy objects yet, so she had nothing but a feeling.

But she wasn't the only one who felt the familiarity.

– *I found them!* A child's voice reverberated. Of course, Aness thought she was hearing things and ignored it.

– *I said, I found my comrades. Why are you ignoring me?!*

The child's voice kept chirping around her ear, but Aness continued ignoring it. Aness had just lost everyone precious to her because of a young prince.

I guess ghosts do exist in this world. But why now?

She didn't think about why she began hearing ghostly voices when she was with these strangers. She just thought that since children do pass away, child ghosts probably existed as well.

– *Argh! Hiss! Damn it!*

What a foul-mouthed ghost, she thought. Perhaps it had a

hard life before it died, or it had a terrible temper from birth.

Pushing the thought aside, Aness spoke out loud. "The people of my house had put in quite an effort to appoint me as the knight of the house."

"Wow, is that right?"

The reason she was answering all these people's questions was simple: She couldn't beat them. And she was indebted to them.

"They didn't approach me after I freed all the horses in the estate into the wild, though."

"Whoa."

A different sort of admiration came in response to her story this time, and it was from Lett, the woman whom she couldn't measure the strength of. But her reactions were appreciative, so Aness enjoyed telling Lett her story.

She's adorable.

Feeling a little more relaxed, Aness smiled. It was a smile that had made many girls at the Capital Academy follow her around, calling her "big sister."

"Wh-whoa…"

At the third sigh of admiration, Charl glanced at Aness. It was an indifferent look, but she felt like she had received a silent warning. Startled, Aness stopped smiling. Then clearing her throat awkwardly, she continued.

"The Kingdom of Noahd had been unstable for a long time, but the foundation crumbled during this generation. It was the source of all the misfortunes that befell them."

Aness' voice became darker as she spoke. Most people would have started to tear up while telling this story, but Aness had never cried like that in all her life. People who were gone never came back, no matter how much they were missed.

Just like her mother.

Aness knew that very well.

That's why I wanted to follow her.

With a brief, bitter smile, she opened her mouth again. "There is only one royal member of this kingdom left in this generation."

"Oh, then?"

Did they see it happen? Aness swallowed a groan as she observed Lett watching the hole that had been closed once the child king was sucked inside. They must have intervened after watching for a while. That made sense. It was more natural than spontaneously jumping in to fight. Still, she was taken aback that they had found out about the hole.

Hiding her bewilderment, Aness nodded calmly. "That is the place that the Fairy King of the Earth, Noahd, left behind." The place that led to the place that Noahd had left behind, to be exact.

"Noahd, huh?"

"The Fairy King of the Earth."

"A fairy, huh?"

Aness felt out of her depth. These people didn't seem surprised. In fact, they seemed more fascinated than shocked.

It's like they truly believe in the fairy king. Why, though?

Aness blinked dazedly.

SIDE STORY
CHAPTER SIX

"Should we have brought our babies?" Lett asked her husband with a frown.

Charl kissed her between her brows. "No."

Babies? Did she say babies? I guess they are a married couple with kids.

Aness' thoughts didn't last long.

"If we brought them here, they would have rambled about the fact that there was another fairy king here."

"Yeah, which is why I think they would have been happy to be here."

"I suppose it would make you happy to see them excited."

"Of course! They're always scolded and told to restrain themselves but imagine how happy they would be if they could use their fairy powers unhindered."

Lett's face glowed endearingly as her eyes sparkled, causing Aness to pause, even in her confused state. The more she listened, the stranger it seemed.

It sounds like her babies are fairies...?

Aness hunched her body in a way she never usually did. She had always avoided a certain type of person—a mentally insane person—throughout her entire difficult life. She wondered desperately how she could get away from these people, never once thinking that they were speaking the truth.

"What are you guys talking about?" asked a pink-haired man who appeared out of nowhere, in a lazy voice.

"Oh, you're back."

"Yeah. There was one fool who refused to leave until the end."

"There's a human being who wouldn't run away after seeing Lady Fletta's monstro—I mean, incredible ability?"

"Chancellor, the lady is glaring at you."

The rest of the group greeted the pink-haired man as if it was the most natural thing to do, but Aness stared at him, bewildered.

Where did he come from? She then remembered that he had been with the others when they first appeared. *But where has he been all this time? Why is he here now?*

Wait. He said that there was one man left out there.

Aness dazedly regarded the wall of dirt that had been created by Lady Fletta. The wall that she had produced by slamming her fist against the ground was now shielding them from the pursuers, so they would have no idea what was happening on this side.

I thought they were all gone.

"Who was the one that was still here?"

"The, uh… the chairman? I think that's what she called him."

Aness' eyes widened at his words. *Yes, he's overly responsible, so he wouldn't have left easily.*

The pink-haired man walked toward Aness, sat down, and proceeded to stare at her. His pink eyes looked like flower petals.

If fairies were real, I bet they would look like him.

Just as the thought drifted into her mind, the man with the pink hair asked, "So, that's what a fairy king left behind?"

"I thought you asked what we were talking about. You heard everything, Baba!"

His name must be Baba. Even his name sounds magical. Is he the reason the others didn't react much to the talk about fairies? No, even though he is fairy-like…

"This is problematic," Baba said, cutting through her thoughts. "We need to hurry up and deal with this. Why are you guys so relaxed?"

"Deal with what?" Aness tensed as she unconsciously repeated his words, and the man waved his hand as he turned to her.

"Oh, it's nothing malicious. I literally meant dealing with something, like work.'"

"I think saying it like that would make her even more nervous, Baba."

"I don't know. You guys tell her then." Looking completely blank and unmotivated, Baba stood up and slumped down next to Clover. And to Aness' indignant surprise, no one explained what "deal with" meant; instead, they absurdly began talking about fairies again.

"It's fascinating that we found traces of a fairy king here, isn't it? I really think I should call for them."

"Do we get to see the fairy kings then?"

"Chan—I mean, Clover. You were absolutely over the moon about my babies before. Why are you so indifferent now?"

"The only one who was over the moon was that coun—Ruman jerk. I only see them as troublemakers now."

"I want to see them!" Lady Fletta yelped. "The fairy kings!"

"Right? Of course, you would! As expected of Greengold!"

"It's Peridot! Lady Peridot Fletta! Why are you like this when you know what my name is now?"

"Ah, finally. This is the lady I know. It was kind of awkward seeing you so good-tempered." Lett grinned playfully as she watched Lady Fletta quiver in front of her.

Charl was gazing sweetly at Lett. He seemed so blinded

by love that Aness wondered if his world was just made up of Lett and vice versa.

Her lips parted slightly as she watched the group. She didn't know where to begin, and her head was in shambles.

Basically, they're here to "deal with" something, but it doesn't seem unrelated to me.

That was what nagged at her the most, but she was being hit with a deluge of other information that bothered her.

That lady is a noblewoman, then, but she's taking care in her speech toward the others. Is it because she is younger than them? Or because the others hold higher positions?

But it seems like something more than that. She's oddly courteous towards them.

The difference in their status became clearer when Aness saw the lady's look of contrition after shouting at Lett.

Which means Lett and Charl are more like masters to the lady, at least.

Even the man, Clover, acted differently toward them. There was only one status a noble would consider to be their master.

Now that I think about it, their faces are similar to the drawings I've seen of the people in the West Continent.

The West Continent... the... Kalior...

Aness tried hard not to continue her thoughts and tore

her eyes away to look at Baba instead. If those two were who she thought they were, then who was this man who treated them so casually?

I wonder if he's a head priest...?

Goosebumps prickled her arms. It was a random thought that had popped into her head, but it was plausible.

ness gulped again and then recalled the third piece of flabbergasting information. Information that seemed so outrageous that she addressed it last.

Fairy kings? Fairies? Real, live fairies?

"Wait! Hold on a moment." Aness' hand finally shot into the air. She wanted to appear meek and docile in front of these unknown powerful people, but she felt that she needed to clear some things up.

"Have you truly seen fairies?"

"How peculiar that is what you are curious about." For the first time, Clover agreed with Lady Fletta's comment.

"B-but you said fairies! No, fairy *kings*!"

"Uhm..." Lett blinked for a moment. "Why are you reacting like that? As if you've never seen fairies before."

Of course, I've never seen one! Who the hell lives with fairies? Are we in a fairytale? That was what she wanted to scream, but Aness managed to shove down those words at the menacing look in Charl's eyes.

"I apologize for my rudeness."

"No, no, I was just surprised."

The gears in Aness Dunn's head shifted as she thought of what to say next. "Then, I wonder if I could perhaps receive help from the fairy kings."

"Hmm. What sort of help?" Lett asked, smiling mysteriously. She was the friendliest of all of them, but Aness tensed when she saw her face shift a bit.

When she felt an indescribable pressure come over her, she was certain that this woman's aura was indeed different. The way she could control it however she wanted and use it to influence others made Aness certain that her powers were as strong as Charl's.

These people couldn't be insane. They were most likely...

"Our kingdom has another relic of a fairy king. It is said that the fairy king was in the image of an elf. Even his name remains to this day, so he is the fairy that the people of our kingdom know the best."

Well, it was the legend people knew best. But if the legends were true...

"Ooh, what was his name?"

"They say it was Chen Christ."

"I've never heard it before. The name sounds quite human for a fairy's name, though."

"That's why many believe him to be an elf or a human rather than a fairy king. That's the most widely accepted theory. Except..." Aness turned her gaze to the hole that she had shoved the young king through. She stared at it for a moment, before giving a hollow laugh. "Chen Christ left behind a 'Bell of the Winds' that can temporarily chase away the insurgents of this kingdom when it is rung."

And the royal authority would be recovered in a flash. These lands were built with the blessing of the fairies, so that was possible. No matter how rotten it had become.

"One must sneak into the royal palace and pass through all the entryways that the fairy king himself created to toll the bell. Not a single soul has successfully passed them. But perhaps the fairy kings could."

If the bell was rung, the young prince's life would be safe until he could be crowned as the rightful king. And perhaps the fairy kings could help protect the kingless throne during the ten years he needed to spend in training. If that wasn't possible, then maybe he could at least travel freely between that prison of a hole and the palace...

Either way, my work would be complete.

Aness thought she wouldn't be ashamed to see her friends again if she could at least achieve that. She didn't have any attachment to this world that had snatched away every single loved one from her. Death would be a relief.

"So, you want us to interfere in this kingdom's civil war?" Lett's question interrupted Aness' thoughts. "Hmm. And what will you give us in return?"

"I shall actively cooperate with whatever you have to 'deal with' regarding myself," Aness replied, thinking of the power that she didn't use often because it was oddly difficult to control. "I shall be as useful as I can be in every aspect."

Lett's expression changed as she tried to suppress her laughter, her eyes gleaming as she glanced from Charl to Clover, Baba, and finally Lady Fletta. Each of them halted at her gaze.

"All right. As long as you cooperate. Oh, I should call for my babies, then. Are we all on the same page now?"

"If that's what you wish, Lett." Charl chuckled and lightly kissed her cheek.

The others either gazed at the pair wistfully and laughed, sighed, or looked disgusted—*but why*—and nodded in agreement.

Aness was dumbfounded by the way things had worked out for her so easily, but then she enthusiastically expressed her gratitude. "Thank you very much! I shall leave everything in your hands!"

And within an hour, she met real fairies.

CHAPTER SEVEN

"Lettie!" The yellow-haired fairy appeared out of thin air. "I missed you! Where did you go?"

Then, a red-haired fairy and a blue-haired fairy shrieked "Lettie!" as they rushed to her.

"Th-the real fairies!"

Aness stood there in shock, her mouth hanging open as she stared at the fairies who looked like young boys. The only things that matched her expectations were their wings. Everything else completely surpassed even her wildest imaginations.

It was as though each fairy was screaming, "This is my color!" with the entirety of their bodies. Their eyes matched their hair, and their facial expressions somehow matched their color. Even their lips appeared to give off a tinge of whatever color they represented.

Could it be that they changed their lip color to the color they liked...?

Arriving at the correct answer without realizing it, Aness blinked rapidly.

"Hmm? Who's that?" The yellow fairy king, or Nell,

tilted his head when he saw Aness. His eyes, which looked like two pieces of amber, glittered with a mysterious shine. His blond hair was closer to the color of melted amber than gold. It all looked sweeter than honey, and her first impression of Nell and his slightly droopy eyes was that he looked very endearing.

"This is my new friend."

Friend? Aness scoffed at Lett's words, and Nell's lower lip protruded.

"She's not Lettie's friend!"

"Yeah! She says she isn't!"

When did I say that? It was true that she and Lett weren't friends, but she couldn't help but feel surprised because she had never said that out loud.

"Oh, it isn't that. She just doesn't know it yet."

"She doesn't know she's your friend, Lettie?"

"Yup!"

Excuse me.

But Aness didn't get the chance to nitpick. These fairies were talking right in front of her eyes, having appeared in a cloud of shimmering dust, armed from head to toe in mysteriousness.

"She's a dummy!"

"Hehehe! You're right! A dum-dum!"

"Don't say things like that. Those are bad words."

"Okie. We'll only use the words you say, Lettie!"

"Stupid!"

Lett had apparently used that word in front of the boys—or rather, the fairy kings—before and was now sputtering, unable to chastise them for it.

It was the advent of a myth, but it was far from what Aness had imagined. Her face twisted oddly.

For now, she studied the fairy kings, who were denying the mysterious legends with their entire existence. To begin with, they were practically naked. The clothes they wore were made of a material that was opaque, pure white, and fluttered lazily in the wind, the way it was described in tales about golden children. That was magical in itself, but...

They weren't wearing anything else.

I suppose that kind of attire is fitting on their continent. According to the myths in Aness' country, the fairy king had covered his skin with extravagant clothing.

Even the way they rushed to Lett—as if they might have stampeded toward her on their chubby legs if not for their wings, rubbing their cheeks on hers as they embraced her— was so strange that it blew her mind.

At least their physical visages were so mysterious and beautiful that it truly made her realize that they weren't humans. The other fairies were Bell, whose hair was as red as the brightest apple and had ruby-red irises. And Gill, who held the clearest blue sky in his hair and waved whenever his hair fluttered. Their bright colors contrasted with their pearly white skin, which made them unimaginably enigmatic and exquisite.

"Stupid!"

But the way these boys—no, these fairy kings—were acting was...

"Seriously, boys!"

"Give it up, Lett. It's not like it's a bad word."

"Yes, it is! Aness isn't stupid!"

"Then to whom may they say that word?"

"They can say that to you, Clover, when you curl up in the street to sleep because you feel like walking home is a waste of time."

"How can you say that when you're the one who gave me the sleeping bag?"

"Obviously, I gave it to you so you wouldn't freeze to death because I'm in no position to stop your stupidity!"

"Oof!"

"Stupid, stupid! There's a stupid right there!"

"Ehehehe!"

Aness felt like she had seen something like this before.

Yes... It's like I'm looking at the little brats who didn't want to be separated from their mothers. She had seen children like this when she was at the Academy. That was how the first years were.

Incredible little troublemakers, they were... But I'm glad they weren't affected by the incident of treason.

Aness blinked as she brushed away the thoughts of her juniors from her younger days, to whom she had been attached. Now wasn't the time for leisurely reminiscences.

"So, these are the, uh..."

"Oh, yes, Aness. These are my babies!"

"Babies..." Aness' voice trailed. They looked at least twelve, so calling them "babies" was kind of...

She swallowed hard and forced herself to greet them. "Greetings, fairy kings." She bent her waist at a ninety-degree angle because she wasn't sure of the proper way to greet them, but laughter echoed around her.

"Lettie! She bowed to us!"

"Weird! That's weirdly weird!"

"Hiii!"

Though they looked to be in their early teens, the fairies laughed like little children. *They're so pure.* With that thought in mind, Aness tried to read them further.

Lett looked like she was stifling her laughter, too. "Y-you

don't have to bow like that. Please stand up."

"She's right. Those fairies are just little rascals who grow flowers in the garden."

When Aness turned to glance at Clover grumbling in a corner, she saw Lady Fletta glancing over with sparkling eyes, looking ecstatic.

"Fairies! Real, actual fairies! How beautiful!"

Aness could almost feel the insanity radiating from her. *Perhaps she's just in shock?*

"You should straighten up before they build a pyramid with their bodies on your back," Charl said curtly as he watched on.

Aness quickly stood up, feeling some kind of comfort that there was at least one other person who was as surprised as she was.

"Shall we get a move on, Lett?"

"Yes, let's go."

Aness didn't need to explain or request anything else. After a vague round of introductions, the party began heading toward the capital.

"As I mentioned earlier, there is an entryway over—"

Boom.

"Whoa, Lady Fletta! How did you do that? Your control was impeccable!"

"Well, no, I was trying to knock down the door, but the entire entrance collapsed."

There was no need for Aness to explain where the entranceways that the fairy king had left were. The party, which had begun its raid in the middle of the night, cast soundproofing spells around them and literally burst through each gateway as they moved along. Their destructive power was monstrous.

Lady Fletta's superhuman strength wasn't the only power, either.

"Hmm, this gate melts under moonlight. Oh, the God of the Moon says it's a power he hasn't seen in a while. This must have been left behind by a fairy king."

"I see."

"If this is truly the power of a fairy king, then I wonder which domain the fairy king that looked like an elf ruled over?"

Everyone pondered Clover's question before giving their responses.

"Loners? The protective god of loners."

What did that even mean?

Aness gazed at Lett in disbelief, pausing in the middle of sheathing the sword she had taken out to help.

"I thought he might like hiding away, seeing all these

protective gateways blocking our way. My babies all have different personalities based on their elements, too.”

“Hmm...” Unbelievably, Charl nodded sagely at Lett’s completely nonsensical words. “That makes sense.”

“How does that make sense?” Clover shouted, looking aghast.

“A hermit fairy king. Wouldn’t it be possible?” The lady of terrifying strength corrected the word “loner” to “hermit,” which sounded much better.

“Oh, yeah! Hermit! That’s perfect!”

No! Aness intervened, unable to just stand and listen. “Didn’t the legends say he was the Fairy King of the Winds?”

“Did they? Hermit sounds much more interesting.”

Aness clenched her fists at Clover’s mutterings. Just as she relaxed enough to walk closer to the party, the voice that she’d heard inside her head began to shout again.

– What did you bring along with you? Escape from there at once! Damn it all, what a useless vessel!

She heard the voice right as they smashed, melted, and walked past five entranceways.

– Why have my comrades been saved by them, of all people? Are you listening to me? At least show me some kind of reaction! I’ll go berserk if you keep ignoring me!

Berserk? Aness’ reaction was far from dramatic, but the

voice seemed delighted.

– That's right! Just like that girl's holy object—no—her god is doing! I wonder why he's so downcast, though...

"Hmm..." Aness glanced at Lady Fletta and cocked her head.

It appeared that the voice belonged to the power that she had received recently.

A power that talks? No, the voice had said "holy object." So... a power within... an object?

"An ego sword?" That was the only thing that came to mind, and she murmured it out loud.

Charl glanced back at her. "The object you hold is not an ego, but an object that houses a god."

"Oh, can you hear a voice, then?" Lett said.

Aness nodded involuntarily and was startled to see that they had the exact same smiles.

"Birds of a violent feather indeed... What are they scheming now?" Clover grumbled once more.

Aness, who had never been frightened by anybody before, gulped. Her instincts were screaming at her again.

Screaming at her to do exactly as they said.

SIDE STORY
CHAPTER EIGHT

"How well can you control your power?" Lett gave a smile as she asked.

"I have only used it a few times." Aness swallowed hard. "My power is related to shadows."

"Shadows, huh."

"I can swallow a body with its shadow. I can't kill it immediately, but I can suffocate it over time."

"I see."

That was one of the reasons Aness didn't use her power often. The nature of the ability didn't suit her as a knight. She hadn't even used it as a last resort because the dark power might do more harm than good in protecting the king.

It feels so ominous.

Despite all of this, she wasn't afraid, which was why she was ignoring the voice that still whispered in her ear.

"It hasn't been long since I started hearing the voice."

"Interesting."

"It's a ghost! A ghost!"

"Nuh-uh! Ghosts don't exist. They're all fairies!"

"No! We're the only fairies!"

"Boys, where's Glenn? Why are only you three here?"

"Is a secreeet!" The fairies taunted like unruly children. Lett scoffed as they shook their heads and dashed toward an unbroken gateway.

"Should I capture and drag them back here?"

"No, it's all right." She shook her head in response to Charl's menacing question.

Baba, who had been watching on silently, piped up, "Things will be easier with the fairies here." He was observing Aness and Lady Fletta. "Shadows and superhuman strength... You know, we're inside the ancient relic of a fairy king, so the powers of gods are that much weaker."

"Is that so?"

"Yes. If they eat up all the fairy dust, then we can deal with those holy objects of low caliber. Or we could probably make the gods sleep or tame them. Those children aren't regular fairies, but fairy kings, so I think it's certainly possible..."

"What?! We'd be able to keep the holy objects, then? Why didn't you say so earlier?"

"It's worth a try since we're inside a fairy king's ancient artifact. Also, the powers aren't strong enough to be considered hostile, and given their current state, a fairy king's power should be greater. It wouldn't have taken so long for me to deal with the two humans earlier if I'd known a place like this existed."

Aness blinked. "I don't really want to retain this power—"

"It would be more convenient for you if you did. At least for protecting your young king," Charl commented indifferently.

Even Clover and Lady Fletta, who were smashing an entranceway up ahead, nodded in agreement.

Aness clamped her mouth shut. She couldn't bring herself to say she was thinking about dying once she found somewhere safe. She instinctively knew she shouldn't, and she finally understood.

The reason these people were helping her to this extent was because they wanted her *with* her power.

Maybe not, but... She had never tolerated anyone who had tried to use her before, so why was it different now? That was the only thing that bemused her.

"What a shame! Why does my god always make me take the difficult way around? Hmm? What was that? All right, stop with the excuses right there..."

Putting Baba, who was mumbling to himself in his hazy voice, behind her, Lett strode energetically toward Aness. She squeezed Aness' hand when she flinched in surprise. Her ruby eyes sparkling, Lett asked, "Could you show me your power?"

"Oh..."

"I'll show you mine if you show me yours."

Aness couldn't stop her body from quivering at her grin.

"This is my power." Lett vaguely waved her hand, and little torches appeared along the underground path that had previously only been lit by the glow of the fairies.

Whoosh, whoosh!

Torch after torch appeared, lighting the corridor with the entranceways as bright as day. A warmth melted into Aness' body. Feeling a sense of stability within her heart, she looked past Lett and froze.

Two torches hit a ghastly monster that had been stirring behind the next gateway, and the monster writhed in agony before melting away.

Gulp. Aness stared blankly at the sight for a moment and then nodded vigorously.

"I-I shall show you my power."

My sister is dead.

Her hair brushed the ground. Matching blue irises could be seen between the strands of her dirty, matted blue hair.

Ylavia stared at the dark, dilated pupils as she stood, rooted to her spot. Those eyes that had been praised as blue diamonds were now empty and unable to see her.

The people in the street whispered among themselves as they passed by.

"It appears the House of Duke Selviers has fallen. Treason, of all things."

"The lady had commissioned the assassination of Archduke Toriah. How frightful!"

Ylavia's sister, Ysette, had died a criminal guilty of treason—the crime of crimes.

Calling it treason was ridiculous. Archduke Toriah wasn't the ruler of the kingdom in the first place. However, there was no longer anyone left to point that out.

They said he was going to be the emperor now. Who would have thought the ancient royal family would crumble so easily?

If my sister really had hired an assassin, she'd have made the right decision.

The young king, who had vanished, and Lady Aness Dunn, who had disappeared with him, were the only ones in favor of the royal family now. Everyone else, like her sister, had...

They're all dead.

That was the only news that her close friends from the Academy had managed to convey to her.

"It isn't surprising. There were a lot of rumors about that lady."

"Rumors?"

"Oh, yes. She was famous for being venomous."

No, that isn't true.

"There are also rumors that she didn't hire an assassin but tried to use poison. She was very educated about poisons, you know. I believe that's more plausible."

Criminals guilty of treason were left to hang in the streets for a week.

But they said my sister was going to hang for a single day.

Ylavia barely managed to tear her eyes away from her sister to look at the signpost pounded into the ground next to her.

"Ysette Selviers.

This criminal has abandoned her honor as a noble and has committed unforgivable crimes.

First, she has uttered countless lies in the presence of the soul of the Great Fairy King.

Second, she has provided asylum for traitors.

Third, the archduke...

Thus, she must be subject to rightful punishment,

but taking the verity that she is the daughter of a loyal subject into consideration…"

How could the archduke do this to her? She was his fiancée. How could he have killed her in such a cruel manner? Her execution had been hasty and enforced earlier than the scheduled date.

"I knew she would end up like this. She was a completely evil wench."

Evil wench?

Ylavia forced her lips to stop trembling. With shaking hands, she bent down and picked up the bag she had involuntarily dropped. She thought she might collapse, but she stiffened her back and slowly turned around.

The whispers fell further behind her.

The mansion she had not returned to in a decade looked as though it had been abandoned for years.

Ylavia recalled her sister's vacant, dead eyes and shuddered. But she didn't have to think about them for long. Someone silently came up to her and stood by her side.

"Welcome home, Lady Ylavia."

Hans had been the butler of their house for a long time. He was the only one who had taken care of the two sisters when they were young. But that, too, was such a long time ago.

"It has been ten years, my lady."

"Yes..." She forced herself to answer and then turned her eyes away from his gray hair. "Where is my father?" she asked in a strangled whisper.

Looking upset, Hans replied, "He is waiting for you."

"Lead me to him."

"This way, my lady."

The sound of her heels echoed loudly. The hallways of the estate were quieter than she remembered. She didn't see a single servant in the entire time she followed Hans.

"The head maid, Anna; the housekeeper, Sue; and I are the only ones left here," Hans said in a low voice, noticing Ylavia looking around surreptitiously. "The master has sent the rest away, saying no good will come to anyone with ties to this family."

"I see." Ylavia kept her eyes forward as she replied indifferently. She didn't have to ask further. All the servants had probably scattered after receiving hefty sums.

One thing kept nagging at her though. Ylavia didn't know the details of what exactly had happened because the news from the Academy had traveled to her late.

Why was Ysette's execution date moved up? The archduke

had kept her alive all this time, unlike the other older students. *So why did he kill her in such haste suddenly?*

She was a traitor. That had to be the only answer.

I heard that Aness escaped with the king. They must have been unable to capture her.

The two sisters had grown up with their temperamental yet virtuous father. There was no way Ysette would have conspired to poison or assassinate anyone, even if she had been forced into this circumstance. If that was the case, then there had to be evidence that tied her to treason, which would mean...

Ysette did something in relation to their escape.

Ysette, Aness, and several other older students—their group of almost ten—were considered heroes by many of the younger ones. So much so that the younger students had always shared news about them even after they had graduated from the Academy. Their group had protected the young king together.

If Aness and the king are dead, then there's absolutely no hope. However, if they're alive...

The official announcement was that they had been killed, but Aness' head hadn't been displayed like those of the other traitors. Ylavia was certain the archduke had failed.

So, what should we do?

Stopping her thoughts from continuing further, she straightened her back even more.

Right now, father is the important person to focus on.

"I'm worried about my father."

At Ylavia's calm statement, Hans let out a faint sigh. They continued walking down the hallway.

Duke Selviers appeared to have aged thirty years, not ten.

"I have returned, father."

"That you have."

Ylavia approached the man she had hated for years but yearned for at the same time. She embraced him tightly, burying her head in his shoulder. She had never been this close to her father before. The man who had been so strict and incredibly daunting was now terribly thin.

Her father stiffened in surprise and then carefully wrapped his arms around her. "Welcome... welcome home."

Ylavia gritted her teeth when she felt her father's soundless sobs. She knew he desperately loved his children, despite their complicated childhoods. She remembered the moment her rigid father had carefully embraced her and her sister after being at a loss for what to do.

While she had resented him, she had never, ever, thought

to drive a stake through his heart like this.

Ysette had probably felt the same.

Sob.

The day the traitor Ysette died, the family members who were left behind wordlessly comforted each other. And that night, Ylavia tightened her jaw as she resolved to make everything right, no matter what she had to do.

After a mere week had passed…

"What did you say?"

"Well, my lady, shockingly, there is no longer any trace of them…"

She received the news about the gateways that the Ancient Fairy King had left.

CHAPTER NINE

In short, Aness Dunn's power was useful.

"It's an arrow?" I muttered, fascinated.

Aness nodded. "Yes, and if I combine the bow with it, then..."

"Ooh, it's a spear!"

"Y-yes, that's right. It becomes a spear."

"And that's the power of the autumn night! Right? Priesty?" Gill asked.

"That is correct. You are amazing, dear fairy king," Baba answered in a drowsy voice, and Gill giggled.

"The autumn night?" I asked, rubbing Gill's head.

Unexpectedly, it was Clover who answered. "I have heard about the God of the Autumn Night before."

"Yes, a mid-tiered god who is closer to being high tier."

"Where did you get that information?"

"He appears in ancient texts sometimes."

I leaned into Charlemagne, and he laughed softly before picking me up and placing me on his shoulders, which I could sit on because they were so wide. As I giggled, I saw Lady

Peridot watch us for a moment before she shifted her gaze to the chancellor.

Huh?

Then, she silently measured his shoulders with her eyes before turning her head away. It happened so suddenly that the chancellor didn't seem to have noticed, but everyone else did.

Well, except for my babies. Anyway, does this mean they have a little something going on?

My proud smile widened, and Clover, after being lost in thought, turned to me and twitched in surprise.

"What are you thinking about? Why are you grinning so mischievously?"

"What was that?"

"N-nothing..."

Please spare my life. He shrank away, muttering to himself.

As we moved along, the conversation shifted to how the God of the Autumn Night specialized in making things rot away.

Finally, we made it to the end of the corridor.

"Aw, we're here already," I grumbled and climbed down from Charlemagne's shoulders, and he hugged me from behind, also feeling sad that the corridor had ended. Holding on to his arms, which were locked around me, I glanced at the others, who looked just as disgruntled as Clover.

"Do we now ring that bell?"

"Yes," Aness said. She looked quite fearful of us and tried her best to smooth out her disgusted expression.

The bell doesn't look that special. There was nothing beautiful about it, nor did it have any special aura.

However, the fairies had been silent for a while, as if they felt something different. They whispered to each other, and I could hear them wondering if they should wake Glenn and make him come over.

I looked at Aness. "You should be the first to ring the bell."

Aness let out a long sigh and then bowed respectfully to me. "Thank you for your consideration."

"Of course. How long do you have to strike it, though?"

"Most likely for at least half a day. It may take that long to inhibit the movement of the rebel army."

"I see. That's the effect of this bell, then?"

Wait, but that meant that it would be exhausting for one person to ring it.

"Do you want to give it a go?" Charlemagne asked after laying a kiss on my lips. I crinkled my nose in a smile and nodded. He laughed and cast his eyes over the bell. "It appears your turn will come soon, so you can ring it to your heart's content then."

"Do you want to try, Charl?"

"I'll listen instead."

"Lady Aness hasn't even begun, though," Clover muttered, listening to our conversation.

"Leave them be. I'm sure Lett can whack away at it all day."

"All day, Baba? You sound so sure of yourself."

Even Aness was only estimating. Baba twitched.

"You'll go after me, then, okay?"

"Fine," Baba replied limply. It looked like the God of the Sun had told him something.

Whatever the case, hitting the bell would help this kingdom, which was fortunate.

Eventually, Aness began ringing the bell. The moment she struck the bell, everyone held their breath, even Charlemagne, who pricked up his ears to listen carefully.

The sound was so delicate and so sorrowful that the word "ring" couldn't dare describe it. It felt like a longing for a homeland that it couldn't return to. No, more than longing or wanting to return... the sound seemed to wish to sing about the beauty of that place. Those who heard it couldn't help but hold their breath at the raw emotions that swept over them.

The only beings that didn't...

"Sniffle."

"Let's bring our baby brother. *Hic.*"

"Yeah, let's do that. *Sob.*"

Only the fairies spoke over the sound that vibrated deep within our hearts. Their voices didn't clash with it, but rather harmonized as one. For the first time, their baby voices sounded beautiful.

Gill wiped his teardrops on my sleeve and snapped his fingers. Glenn appeared by their side.

Why is he asleep?

Before I could ask, Glenn twitched and opened his eyes.

"No! No wakey! Our presen—Oh yeah! It's a secret."

Smack!

What did I just see?

My mouth fell open as I watched Glenn fall back asleep— or rather, be forced unconscious—as soon as he opened his eyes, helped by Nell's blow to the back of his head.

After about two hours of ringing the bell, I saw Aness grow weary and sob as she hit it.

The sound of the bell must be stirring her quite a bit. She didn't seem like a person to weep like that.

Aness struck the bell with all her strength, her eyes reflecting deep yearning for *something* as she bawled. It appeared she was mentally drained rather than physically exhausted, like she would dissolve in tears at any moment.

I watched her in silence before looking around at the others. Then, I became certain.

That bell has the power to stop people, but does the bell also intensify the longing that people have in their hearts?

It was a highly plausible assumption.

I thought he was the Fairy King of the Wind, though. What does this phenomenon have to do with the wind?

However, it was soon revealed that I had misunderstood.

Charlemagne, who seemed like his emotions had never been shaken in the first place, spoke to me. "This is the sound of magic being bound."

"Magic? I can't feel it."

"It's binding every power other than that of a holy object. And the powers the fairies have, apparently."

"Aha… That's why they said its power inhibits people. But it looks like Aness can't keep it up in her state."

"I think it's your turn now." Charlemagne gave me a slight smile as he lightly pushed my back.

I nodded gravely and walked toward the bell amidst the others' anxious stares—*why though*—as they slowly collected themselves.

"Aness."

She turned to me, and as her darkened irises met mine, I

hugged her tightly. She flinched, and I patted her back a few times before speaking tenderly.

"I'll take it from here. Go sit down and get some rest."

"Th-thank you." She gazed at me and then slowly lowered her head toward me before the sound of the bell disappeared.

A moment later, I picked up the mallet, and...

Bing! Bing! Bong! Bing! Bing! Bong! Bing! Bing! Bing! Bing! Booong!

I began hammering away at the bell, feeling immensely altruistic and hoping to ease the sadness of those who were feeling down because of the effect of the bell.

My, my! Such self-sacrifice. I'm so proud of myself!

Drunk on the sacred feeling, I played dozens of songs with the bell.

Comfort I give you, dear kingdomers!

"Please... make her stop..." Lady Peridot begged. Her eyes were shaking, but the chancellor avoided looking at her.

"We would have if we could. It's no use."

"But..." Even Aness, who had been bawling, looked flabbergasted as she listened to the sound of the bell.

The sacred sound was now ringing like the bell at the

end of a school day.

"Hum! Hum! Hum! There's only one!"

Oh, there are lyrics, too.

Lady Lett was shaking her bottom delightedly, almost dancing to the tune.

Baba grinned. "She probably won't get tired because she can use the power of her holy object properly now. Just give up…"

The way he was standing with his hands clasped behind his back was aggravating, but not as much as the behavior of His Majesty, Emperor Charlemagne. He was deeply engrossed in the absurd bell performance, as though he was watching an angel sing. The chancellor pointed toward their emperor and shook his head, the bags under his eyes nearly reaching his chin.

Lady Fletta accepted the situation and sat down.

"What are you doing?" Clover asked, watching her settle comfortably on the ground.

"Might as well enjoy it, then. Fortunately, the sound of the bell is lovely, so it doesn't seem it will hurt our ears even if we listen to it all day."

Clover stared at her like she was something else, and then let out a deep sigh as he slumped heavily down next to her.

They seem pretty close...

Of course, he had no way of knowing what Baba was thinking.

Meanwhile, thanks to Lett playing "Mary Had a Little Lamb" off-beat, Aness Dunn came to her senses. And when the music transitioned into Beethoven's Symphony No. 3...

Aness leaped to her feet, the light shining in her eyes again.

CHAPTER TEN

That incident happened before the rumors that the entrance-ways had been destroyed had even spread all the way across the kingdom.

"The bell is ringing."

Ylavia staggered to the front doors of the estate, hauling them open and stepping out into the front yard. She walked and walked, following the sound of the bell. It was the first time she'd heard it, but she knew.

The fairy king's blessed ones... The people of the kingdom had spread their roots in this homeland over generations.

Yes, I know this sound.

It wasn't because she had heard it before. It was that she had longed for it. She had yearned for it for such a long time without even knowing it. She instinctively realized that the blood of the people of this land had ached for the sound.

"Oh..." Tears dripped down her face, but the feeling didn't last long.

"Ylavia!

"Lavi!"

"Hey! What are you doing outside?"

Her fellow classmates, who had all become listless after losing all but one of their older alumni, were running toward her. Ylavia's eyes widened in surprise.

"How? Why aren't you at the Academy?"

"We followed you right after you left."

Ylavia saw the carriage that had brought them here drive away. Her classmates surrounded her before she knew it.

"We can't lose you and Aness too..." the words that her calm friend uttered were unexpected. "That's why we came, and the bell..."

Ylavia couldn't help but nod as she gazed into the silent but excited eyes of her friend.

"Yes, the bell rang."

They were all magic users, and they had noticed the power of the sound at once.

"We looked around on our way here. We aren't the only ones."

"Yeah."

"And we're the only ones who can move freely in this current situation."

It seemed like everyone had resolved to do something, and Ylavia had a feeling she knew what that something was.

"We need to find His Majesty."

"We need to find him before they do, so we can help."

"And so, our seniors can rest in peace."

The sound of the bell melted over them in their determined silence.

We need to find the king.

The tolling bell bound all magic, friend or foe. A barbaric war could erupt at the slightest push, and more civilians might die if that happened. His Majesty had to regain the throne with the sound of the bell before tragedy hit.

Everything was going to be all right once the king returned.

Just as they started to think that the sound of the bell was slowing, a more rhythmical sound began to play.

Bing! Bing! Bong! Bing! Bing! Bong! Bing! Bing! Bing! Bing! Booong!

The group paused for a moment before asking around for information about where Aness and the king were last seen.

A dark shadow followed behind them.

Aness Dunn sprang to her feet, her eyes twinkling again.

"May I leave this place to you?"

As Lady Fletta and Clover blinked at her sudden but determined change, Baba waved his hand lazily.

"Are you leaving? Go on, then. Your power has stabilized."

Lady Fletta and Clover stared in shock at Baba this time.

"Stabilized" means there was no longer any need to worry about her rebellious god going berserk. Lady Peridot hurriedly checked her own power. She could tell if she could control it or not without resorting to breaking something.

Finally, she murmured, "Yes, I can really control it."

"Lady Peridot...!"

"Chancellor!"

Forgetting to hide their true identities, the pair whooped joyfully and fell into each other's arms.

Baba watched them with a cool gaze as they hastily drew apart and turned to Aness. "The God of the Autumn Night has the power to cause rot. You can use it to the best of your ability, so use it well. It should assist you in bringing the young king back outside."

Aness gazed solemnly at the lady and the chancellor, who were awkwardly facing opposite directions in embarrassment.

"Ahahaha! Charl, isn't this beautiful?!"

"You're always beautiful, Lett."

Then, she turned her eyes to the emperor of the West Continent, who only had eyes for Lett, and then to the empress of the West Continent, who was dancing as she rang the bell to play Pachelbel's Canon in D.

A faint smile flittered through Aness' eyes. She bowed politely.

"Thank you."

She was going to find her king and put everything in its rightful place. Once that was done...

I'll go to my loved ones.

Why is this, though? Was it because she had wept as she listened to the sounds of the bell? Could the color of her heart change so much with such a minor act?

A sudden thought crossed her mind. Perhaps her dearest friends wouldn't be so welcoming if she rushed to their side.

I should go to the king first.

To the young king she had imprisoned alone to protect him. To the small child that her friends had given up their precious lives for.

"See you later!"

Aness couldn't help but chuckle at the yelp from Lett, who was still banging away at the bell like she was far from exhausted.

"Yes. I shall see you afterward."

Looking refreshed and feeling relieved of all her burdens, she turned around and dashed out of the ruins.

Not even an hour had passed when she ran into Ylavia and the other juniors on her way to find the king.

"Why are you here?"

The four juniors froze in place as they watched Aness skid to a stop, and then they rushed to her. They wiped away their tears—Aness scoffed as they didn't wipe with their own clothes—and started shouting.

"The chairman told us!"

"The chairman?" Aness ushered the juniors behind her as she tensed at the shadow they were pointing to.

"Lady Aness."

She smiled coldly at the man who lowered the hood of his robe. "Now, what might our charming chairman be scheming?"

Wasn't he on their side? Didn't he support the rebel forces?

The man gazed at her with an unreadable expression. "I do wish you would stop calling me that."

"Should I call you the young master of the duchy, then?"

"Adehn."

Aness was momentarily dumbstruck. The man smiled hollowly at her and then opened his mouth again, looking as though he might cry.

"You told me before that if I wished to be with you, Lady... no, Aness... that I had to give up everything."

He still looked sorrowful, but also unburdened. His refreshed expression looked like hers.

"Am I too late?"

Aness bit her lip, avoiding his question. "We need to find His Majesty first."

"All right."

Along with the group of younger students, who had been trying to understand what was going on between the two, Aness and Adehn headed to the place where the king was. The power of Aness' holy object rotted away everything in their path, clearing their way.

They stood back-to-back as they defeated a few enemy forces that had arrived before them and approached the entrance of the hole.

"I've rotted the trees to cover our tracks, so we've bought some time."

"Aness, that power…"

"I'll tell you about it later."

Ylavia's eyes sparkled with reverence. "We can hear the bell all the way out here."

Though they didn't say it out loud, they couldn't deny that the irreverent sounds of the bell were giving them strength. It didn't drown them in sadness; instead, it moti- vated them to move for their king.

Crack…

The relic that the fairy king had left so long ago was aging quickly. It couldn't rot, so it merely aged rapidly on its own.

The door crumpled along the annual rings on the wood. It swung open, and a handsome young man walked out.

He looked quite different than before. Luckily, they were able to recognize him as the child king by the color of his eyes and hair. Needing confirmation, Aness drew her blade...

"Aness Dunn."

And immediately sheathed it. She knew that the voice belonged to the king, even though it had completely changed.

"Lady Dunn."

"Greetings, Your Majesty."

"G-greetings, Your Majesty."

"My king."

Aness bent her knees before the king, and everyone followed suit.

The king, who looked to be between a boy and a man, lifted his pale hand in response and turned his eyes in the direction of the royal palace and the gateways.

Ring... Ring... Ring... Ring...

He quietly closed his eyes at the romantic rhythm of the tolling bell. After a while, he spoke.

"Let us go to them. I must see them first."

I have something to tell you.

SIDE STORY
CHAPTER ELEVEN

The young king had remained in the place for only a moment, but he had faced a fragment of the truth in the space of the relic where time flowed rapidly.

Those who have crossed dimensions either are ostracized by the world or discard their previous attributes and melt into it.

The fracture that occurs through this process depends on how far the dimensions are... And as I come from far away, the fracture of this place far exceeded the influence of the gods, and they exploited it.

The words seemed far from reality because they told a story from eons ago, but the young king, who had accepted those words as the authentic truth, thought differently.

The relic was a storehouse of memories.

What kind of beings were the Spirit Kings? How are they able to pass down their intact memories?

The young king didn't yet understand that. The time he was given was too short and had passed too quickly. Even the physical maturing of his body wasn't complete, so it seemed he would transform between his current form and his younger self for the time being. That was why he had to hurry before he turned back into a child.

"Lady Aness?"

The young king took a deep breath as he watched a woman speak the name he could not dare to say. He was able to quell his sorrow only because the time inside the relic had made him neither a child nor a man.

Aness—no, Lady Dunn—probably despised him.

And yet, she was his knight, who had risked her life to protect him.

My knight.

He repeated the phrase a few times in his mind before gazing at Aness, who had led him to those who had saved their lives. The moment their eyes met, she averted her cold gaze.

She still hates me. Of course, she does.

The young king collected himself and turned his eyes to the new people before him.

"Thank you for ringing the bell and helping us."

"Oh, you don't have to thank us. We did it because we needed to." The woman who spoke as a representative of the noble group quickly glanced at Aness.

The king, who had surreptitiously noticed the look, became slightly glum, but not for long. After a few shared greetings of thanks, he cautiously said, "I have something to relay to you."

"What is it?" a brusque man, who he learned was Emperor Charlemagne Kalior, asked curtly.

The young king had already heard about their saviors from Aness on their way here, so he wasn't flustered. In fact, he wasn't even accustomed to being treated as a king, because he had been chased away the moment he sat on the throne. Not to mention that he had attained a greater truth than their identities, which is why he reacted differently than the students of the Academy and the young master.

"The place I was in was a storehouse of memories..." the young king continued calmly. "It holds memories from ancient times."

Everyone was shocked by his story.

"Does that mean that the founders of this kingdom were elves from our country?"

"The founder of this kingdom was the progenitor of the elves, and the first elf that had crossed dimensions to arrive at this place, to be exact."

According to the young king, the first elf was a different species as well as a fairy king. When the others questioned him about how that was possible, he explained that the first elf was the only one who had been both, because he had traveled between dimensions.

"He was the progenitor of elves because he was originally an elf, but he also became something else because he traveled through different dimensions."

Usually, one who crossed a dimension would become another species. However, since he was already of a different species, he had become something even more distinct.

And that was a fairy king.

"Fairy kings are the pillars of everything warped and organized."

Thus, the elf, Chen Christ, who was warped, became a fairy king.

"And those fairies..."

"My babies are the pillars of everything organized."

"Yes. The reason why I had to inform you of this is because I must relay his dying wishes to you."

Words that had only been passed down through memories. There hadn't been two fairy kings in this kingdom, but rather one pillar of everything warped with two powers. And that fairy king had left these words.

"What were his last words?"

"Swallow the stone of fairies and make this world whole."

One side of the group tilted their heads in confusion as a somber silence draped the other side.

The king gravely finished imparting the message.

"The stone must be blood red."

The Empress Lett, who was in a good mood after exercising with the bell, waved her hand, looking cheerful. "You know, we're already perfect."

"We cannot be more perfect than we are now," Charlemagne added as he nodded in agreement.

The king, who had temporarily put aside thoughts of regaining his throne, was slightly taken aback. "I am not saying that you are not perfect, but—"

"You said that the fairy king was the pillar of everything warped, did you not?"

The king was relieved that someone had been listening properly to what he said. It was the pink-haired man who looked vacant, Baba, but his response was even more bewildering.

"The objective of the fairy king of all that is warped would only be to warp things. Additionally, he came to this world through a fracture, and my god is telling me that he was a complete psychopath."

"A-a psychopath?"

Baba began telling tale after tale about the atrocities that the Elf Fairy King Chen had committed with his ability to command spirits. After enjoyably watching the others' faces become more horrified, he turned to his own group, who almost looked bored.

"The craziest thing that he did was to constantly attempt to create the fracture between dimensions again."

Both groups were now speechless in the same manner.

"Absolutely insane. Basically, according to him, a fracture that allows travel between dimensions will open if someone swallows the blood-red fairy stone, and that someone would have to be someone like Charlemagne or Scarlett."

People who had been chosen by holy objects and were the bloodline of the gods, to be exact.

The silence was broken by Chancellor Clover, who muttered to himself coldly.

At that moment...

"Your Majesty!"

The young king's body began to shrink.

Chancellor Clover watched Aness pityingly as she rushed to the king's side and picked him up in her arms. He wondered how much trouble she would go through serving a child as a king. Of course, he was brought right back to his senses at Emperor Charlemagne's words.

"Had the fracture been opened, the one who opened it wouldn't have been safe. This little child is repaying our kindness with ingratitude."

Perhaps serving the child would be better.

"So true! Even if we had tolled the bell because we needed it... How awful of them."

At the words that Charlemagne and Scarlett had uttered with chilling looks on their faces, the young king and his subjects looked horrorstruck, never having meant to offend.

The chancellor flung himself at the emperor and the empress. "Why would you try to cause diplomatic problems? Do you *want* to kill me with this job? Please calm yourselves!"

After watching for a moment, Lady Peridot also threw herself at the empress. "Please calm yourself!" Using the superhuman strength that she could now control, she held the empress back with all her might.

The chancellor would no longer supervise her now that she had a handle on her power, which meant that she would have to go visit him. *I can't have him buried in work every time I visit!* She wanted to at least have conversations with him.

Not realizing that Scarlett was trying hard not to laugh at her desperate screams, Lady Peridot hollered with all her strength, "Please calm yourself, Your Imperial Majesty!"

Due to the lady's shout and the blatant revelation of their identities, which the kingdomers were pretending not to know, their return home was hastened.

"I wanted to genuinely scold them at first, but I acted angrier because the way you two were clinging to us was so funny, you know? Well, I suppose we didn't waste our time, because Aness promised to come live with us as an envoy once her work on the East Continent was finished, right?"

"Yes, Your Majesty, I suppose so…"

Not long after, Lady Aness Dunn brought her husband, who had entirely discarded his family and status, to the empire. She began her stately work on improving the relations between the East and West Continents.

But that was a story for another time.

"I swear, you worry too much. Did you really think Charl and I would attack the king of a different country?"

Though he knew that the empress had specially made laxatives in her pocket, Chancellor Clover didn't acknowledge that and nodded firmly before glaring suspiciously at the emperor standing behind her.

I was more worried you two might kill him, not just attack him.

And, as he expected, the corners of Charlemagne's lips curled upward as he lightly kissed Scarlett's hair.

He truly was thinking about killing the king! Clover thanked the heavens that he had stopped them. *Damn my life. Where*

"Anyway, why has our little Glenn been sleeping for so long? What's wrong with him? Did you guys hit him too hard? How could you hit your little brother?"

"Nuh-uh! Not true!"

"So? Why did you do it?"

"We're gonna send our baby brother back!"

"Why aren't you answering my questions? Where did you learn to be so devious?"

"Devious! Devious? Us? We dunnooo…"

"It's a secret…"

"You can't say it's a secret! Bell, you stupid fairy!"

"Ugh, boys!"

Glenn didn't even wake up as the fairy brothers took turns holding him. He was still sleeping soundly when they vanished with him in their arms.

A few days later, it was finally Scarlett's birthday.

"It's a what?"

"Present! Hehehe!"

"It's a present, Lettie!"

"Yeah… Can you say that again?"

"It's a baby for you!"

They handed her Glenn, who was sleeping inside a flower basket with a bottle in his mouth and a pretty flower-shaped bib under his chin.

That day, the fairy kings spent the entire day being scolded by Scarlett for the first time. Eventually, they were also the first to receive rigid imperial etiquette lessons before any baby imperial highnesses were born.